MW00810893

Light Dawns in Darkness

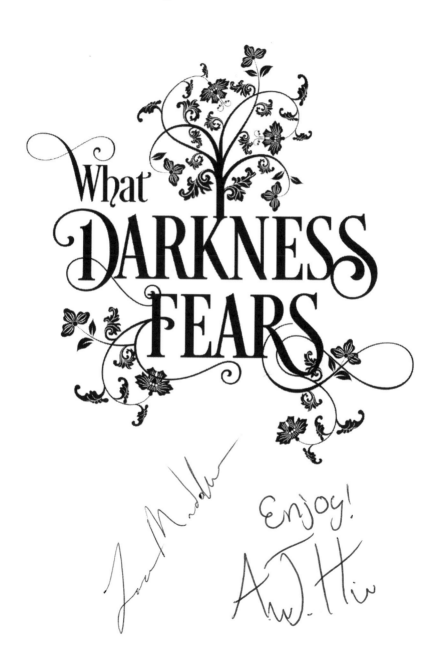

Enjoy!

Praise for What Darkness Fears

"*What Darkness Fears* is the perfect blend of dark and light! Each story is so unique and beautiful, and I found myself pulled into each one. I loved them all! My favorites are probably 'The Headless Henwoman and the Kissing Curse' because it was just so weird and funny and 'The Night Walkers' because it was so cool and creepy! Two honorable mentions are the one with Loki, for obvious reasons, and the one where a writer has to confront their abandoned characters. As a writer with many WIPs set aside, this one hit hard. I like how they all have creepy, dark vibes but end in light, often with a profound message. This is definitely an anthology I'll be reading every year around Halloween and recommend it to readers who like spooky stories without going too far into horror and end well!"

-*Katie Marie, Author of Saving Zora*

"I loved the freshness in each story and poem! It had been my first time reading through an anthology, so I wasn't sure what to expect, but the depth of each piece blew me away and how it contributed to the book as a whole. The spookiness of each of these pieces fascinated and sucked me in—even as I shivered, I couldn't put this anthology down! *What Darkness Fears* is a bright and brilliant anthology by multiple authors, and this will be something I reread every year as it gets closer to Halloween time."

-*Sarah Sutton, Author of If the Broom Fits*

What DARKNESS FEARS

Anne J. Hill • Lara E. Madden • Megan Mullis
Emily Barnett • D.A. Randall • Maseeha Seedat
Beka Gremikova • L.A. Thornhill • Kristiana Sfirlea
Savannah Jezowski • Effie Joe Stock • AJ Skelly
Natalie Noel Truitt • Crystal Grant • Denica McCall
Kat Heckenbach • Laurel Jean

Paperback ISBN: 978-1-956499-00-1
Ebook ISBN: 978-1-956499-01-8

Originally published in October 2021
Published by Twenty Hills Publishing

Cover Art by Psycat Digital Ink & Motion
Cover Edited by Erin Nathanial Design
Paperback Interior Formatting by Effie Joe Stock
Ebook Formatting by Sarah Sutton
Publisher logo by Nathaniel Luscombe

Edited by Anne J. Hill and Andrew Winch,
with help from Lara E. Madden, Crystal Grant,
Katie Marie, Savannah Jezowski,
Laurel Jean, and Emily Barnett
Poems chosen by Megan Mullis

Book created by Anne J. Hill, head of Twenty Hills Publishing,
with the help of Lara E. Madden

All citations of the Bible come from:
New International Version. (2011). BibleGateway.com.
http://www.biblegateway.com/versions/
New-International-Version-NIV-Bible/#booklist

Even in the darkest night, there is hope.
Light dawns in darkness.

To anyone in need of hope
in the midst of despair.

To Anne J. Hill's mom,
a light during many trials.

Contents:

Part Three: In the Dread of Night

"The people walking in darkness
have seen a great light;
on those living in the land of
deep darkness a light has dawned."
-Isaiah 9:2 (NIV)

Introduction

It all started with a conversation. Well, multiple ongoing conversations digging up the purpose of dark stories and why we're drawn to reading and writing them. More importantly, because we are both Christians, we have often talked about how dark stories—and even horror stories—can be used to glorify God.

All quality art has the unique ability to reveal aspects of the human soul that reflect our Creator. We, the creatures, are driven to make beautiful things because He has instilled in us His own personality, sense of wonder, and desire for beauty. But, on a more specific level, why horror? Why scary stories? Why dark fantasy?

Well, we were throwing this idea around, and we unearthed the theme of this book. Our conclusion was this: First, in order to show the whole truth and the hope in a situation—in order to show the *light*—you have to journey to dark places first. Secondly, fear is a human emotion, and dark or scary stories, when they don't pointlessly glorify the darkness, can help us face what we fear. Third, scary stories are *fun!* We remember the things that scare us. We hold on to them. We especially remember the light at the end of the tunnel when the tunnel has been long and perilous. Let's be honest—we're all a *little* bit afraid of the dark. But what does darkness fear? *Light.*

While working on the theme for this book, we did a Bible study on the word "dark." Turns out, that word shows up about 200 times in the ESV translation. Needless to say, there were a lot of verses to dig through. Some had nothing to do with this topic, while others hit the theme head on.

During this, we stumbled on Psalm 112:4, which says, "Light dawns in the darkness for the upright; he is gracious, merciful, and righteous." We'd recommend reading the whole passage for context, but the phrase "light dawns in the darkness" stuck with us and ended up being the inspiration for the tagline.

The Bible is full of darkness. It doesn't shy away from discussing pain, fear, or evil. It doesn't pretend there isn't murder, theft, lying, rape, abuse, demons, death, betrayal, and much more. Instead, it shows the depth of darkness and how dark "simple" things—things like little white lies— really are. But it doesn't stop there. Not at all. It shows the darkness so that it can show the power of our Savior, the Light.

This isn't a new idea. Everyone's heard that there must be darkness for light to shine. Someday, light will shine from every direction, but until then, shadows will remain a part of our daily lives. Some stories and poems circle this theme subtly, while others wield it like a battle axe. But all have a way of striking to the heart of truth.

We are not claiming *What Darkness Fears* to be a revolutionary work of art or to be the scariest horror, the funniest comedy, or the deepest theological exploration you've ever read. It's fun, it's spooky, it's silly, it's odd, and we had a *blast* putting it together.

So, our hope and prayer is that this book will be a light to those in dark places. That it will give you hope and point to God. We hope that it is beautiful, and we hope that it says something true. We hope most sincerely, brave reader, that you enjoy plunging into these stories (and come along for more in the future). May you be transported, amused, and occasionally feel a little chill run down your spine.

-Anne J. Hill and Lara E. Madden

Part One:

A Walk in the Dark

Light Dawns in Darkness
by Anne J. Hill

In the dark, I make my way through winding bends and rustling leaves. The lantern in my hand guides my way. I have a mission here in the dark. Adjusting the strap on my shoulder, I glance down to ensure the letters are secure in my satchel.

I've lost my horse several miles back, but nothing will stop me now. It'd be worse to rest for the night in these woods. Better to continue on foot than to lie in wait and become prey.

The full moon peeks through tree branches losing their leaves in the autumn air. A distant howl makes me pick up my dress and quicken my pace.

"These letters must reach the Emperor! Do you understand? This is our final hope," the duke said earlier today as his bloody hands pressed the satchel to my chest. "Follow the smallest road in Waning Forest. Go quick and stop for nothing."

Those were his last spoken words to me, his ward. But his last thought—which my abilities allowed me to hear as clear as a shout—was, *Light dawns in darkness!*

Unfortunately, only my feeble lantern lights my path, and I've so long to go. I'd have gone by train, the fastest transportation there was, but trains are no longer safe since the war began. No longer under the Emperor's control. Nothing is.

The world has burst into a wild flame ever since he took over the throne.

The candle in my lantern flickers when a gust of wind brushes past, and for a moment, I think I will lose what little light I have. But it regains its strength and presses on through the night, ever my guide. I thank God above because I've already used my last match, and this is my final candle.

I try not to be afraid. Afraid of the dark and the things that live in it. Afraid of what might happen if I don't reach the Emperor in time. Afraid of fires blazing across the world if our ruler can't contain them. They have stirred for centuries—coals smoldering beneath civil unrest and oppressing those of us with powers. The Emperor is the one we've been waiting for to finally stoke the flames, but things have moved too fast.

I know the letters by my side can fight back those flames.

Getting them to him is the trouble. Many have died to bring them thus far. They contain our enemy's plans. Some spy died getting them into the duke's hands, and the duke died getting them into mine.

An owl hoots from branches above me. I shudder when it takes flight, spreading large wings overhead.

I shake my head and focus on my path. I've been trudging on since this morning, but this forest is no small space. It stretches from the duke's mansion, through the graveyard, and all the way to the Emperor's castle. And in the darkness, there is no end in sight.

The dirt path under my feet continues to grow smaller and smaller until I find myself pushing through thickets. My expensive new dress snags on a bush, ripping fabric. I try to ignore the thorns that scrape along my cheeks and arms, tearing at my skin like claws attempting to rip apart our empire's last hope.

I will myself to fight through the pain and march on. Like a soldier in the dark. A soldier in a dress.

Holding my lantern low to the forest floor, I search for the faintest shadow of the path.

And then, there it is, bending around a tree. So I follow it, nose nearly to the ground, until wind whips around me and...

the

     light

         goes

            out.

There is no light in the dark.

The path was hard enough to follow before, but now, standing in the middle of this forsaken forest with nothing but the shadows from the moon to hear me, I scream. I scream because I don't know what else to do. This path was meant to lead me. To show me the way to the Emperor. To save the fate of my kind. This path was meant to end the war raging in our empire and give those like me—those with special abilities—a right to live and breathe and create their own light.

But now, there is no light in the dark.

I don't move because I'd rather stand still than head in the wrong direction. At least here I'm on the path.

The howling I'd heard in the distance returns, but this time, it's no longer distant. The creature's low growl rumbles somewhere off to my right. I imagine a wolf crouching on all fours, ready to pounce and make me his meal.

Something illogical tells me I'm safe if I stand here on this path and wait. But that's absurd.

The growling turns to a snarl and then another howl.

Leaves rustle; panting grows nearer. Fear throws me off of the path. Dropping the dead lantern, I run. Blind, I chase after where I think the path must be and away from the hungry wolf.

I stumble over a fallen tree and scrape both my knees through what's left of my dress. I try to ignore the blood that trickles down my legs and press on. Tears attempt to blur my vision, but there isn't much left *to* blur.

The wolf—I can hear him—picks up his pace and must be only feet behind me.

I know this is the end. The end of me. The end of hope. The end of the world.

I reach for my stalker's mind with my powers and hear, *Get her before the graveyard! So close! Closer!*

I've read wolf minds before, and they never had such organized thoughts like this. Terror sinks in deeper, my feet pounding against twigs. This is no ordinary wolf.

Almost! Almost there!

The wolf snarls, and I can feel his breath as his teeth snap at me. I stumble. Search in vain for—

The path!

Up ahead, faint lights. Lanterns? And then...the graveyard!

The path winds toward that haunted place, lanterns growing with each step and illuminating the forest.

In a few brief strides, I'm faced with a tall gate to the cemetery. I fling it open and yank it shut behind me, overly aware that even its wrought-iron bars won't do much against a *werewolf.*

Hiding behind the gate, the beast and I lock eyes. His teeth shimmer with saliva as he crouches low, a growl rumbling from deep in his chest, and he springs forward.

I scream and stumble away from the gate. But the wolf doesn't get in. Instead, some invisible force throws him to the ground before his claws touch the metal.

He whimpers and falls on his side.

I blink and stare at him as his form slowly shifts from fur to flesh. A man slowly pushes up to his full height, eyes locking back to mine.

A tentative smile spreads across my lips, under-standing dawning. "You can't come in here."

His fingers curl into a fist. "Yes, I can. You are mine any moment I wish."

"Then prove it." I lean forward, staring him down.

He smiles widely and walks around the edge of the graveyard, reaching his hand out and touching the gate. Whatever stopped him before doesn't now, his fingers thrumming across the bars until he finds a spot he likes. He grabs hold and leaps over.

He lands on all fours, grinning up at me. "Nowhere is

safe for you."

My throat tightens, and I grab the satchel closer.

The wolfman saunters over to me, pausing inches from my face. For a moment we share breaths—mine ragged and his rancid. We study each other. The grin on his face intensifies. *She's mine.*

There's no point running now. He's much faster than me. So instead, I watch his hands reach for me. Only his fingers curl like they've slammed into a glass wall. His face twists with confusion.

My feet shift on well-traveled dirt, and as I realize the truth, it's my turn to smile. "You can't get me on the path."

I turn to take in my surroundings, ignoring the wolfman pounding at the air.

Hanging on the cemetery gate is a freshly lit lantern. I reach for it and pull it down. I again have a light in the darkness.

I start up the graveyard hill, seeing the path lead through the home of the dead. I admit to myself that I'm still afraid, and that admission frees me—renews my hope.

The wolfman stalks beside me, growling in his human throat. "You are *mine*. You can't stay on the path forever. You'll step off, and I'll be here."

I run my hand over my satchel and don't give him the pleasure of a response.

Passing through the graveyard's shifting shadows, my feet stay fast to the dirt path. I can see it better here, even in the presence of death.

"You think you're somehow safe? I killed the spy. I killed the duke. And now, I'll kill you," the wolfman growls.

I want to ask why he's siding with those who would want him dead, but I decide it doesn't matter. I'm on a mission and indulging his taunts could prove fatal. So I press on.

Bats flit just above my head, but they're no more dangerous than the wolf while I hold to the path. But the walk upward is strenuous, and my legs tremble from the long journey. Even still, I put one foot in front of the other until I reach the top of the hill, the middle of the cemetery.

And here I lift my lantern, in the light of the full moon, with the forest around me, and see the Emperor's castle just beyond the bottom of the graveyard hill.

The path widens as it nears the castle—a safe escort to my destination. The wolfman has lost. He seems to know it too.

"You've beaten me this time, but I'll be back." He growls one last time before darting back into the woods, but his threats turn to ash in the light.

Fear overtook me for a time, but I'm thankful for it. Without it, I'd have never made it back to the path, to this hill, and then on to the Emperor. And this war would have never ended.

Light dawns in darkness.

People Watchers

by Lara E. Madden

You think you came to this café for coffee. You probably even believe it was your own idea. It's not an unusual thing for you to do.

Can you feel it? That innate sense that you're being watched creeping like spiders up your neck? If you do, you brush off the foreboding with a little jolt of your shoulders. You likely think it's silly. You don't even turn around to see who is in the café with you. You really shouldn't ignore your intuition. A wiser man would know that, but you aren't all that wise.

You sit at your regular table by the window, sipping your drink. A latte. The kind with a leaf drawn in the cream. You watch the pedestrians, the traffic, the homeless man across the street, and as you watch, you take notes on a yellow legal pad. If you were a little more aware, you would have noticed me—the dark-haired, immaculate woman in the opposite corner—studying you. You are the observer, being observed. The people-watcher, being watched. You are a rat that doesn't know it's trapped in a maze.

I sip my black Americano and type notes into my computer. I would love to see what kind of notes *you* take. You can tell so much about an individual based on how they see the people around them. For example, *I* am very practical. I know that you live on 239 W High Street and own three cats, although one doesn't often come out from under the sofa. I know you drive a black 2012 Saab 9-3 Sedan. You have friends over for game night every other Saturday. You still have feelings for an old love interest—Jasmine—and you try not to drink alone because you might accidentally call her at two in the morning. I know you hate your job as an accountant, but your first three books never sold very well, so you can't afford to quit. Oh, and you own only two pairs of shoes because you recently adopted a minimalist philosophy. I also know your running route. I sometimes run it myself.

You worry that others find you dull. You fear you are inconsequential, meaningless, unnecessary. But *I* need you.

I've been writing for an hour in this café. Being in the same places where you spend your time always inspires me. Sometimes I wish I could reach out to you, tell you all about it—I'm sure you would understand, being a fellow writer—but I wouldn't want to risk losing this thing we have. So instead, I slip coupons for your favorite café into your mailbox and find my seat in the corner ten minutes before the time I know you'll be there: on your lunch break, before the café's closing time. The day before the coupon expires, because you're a procrastinator, but a frugal one.

You check your wristwatch and sigh. Your shoulders slump forward as you rub your forehead with the tips of your fingers. Time for you to get back to the office, right? Before you begin to pack up, I close my laptop, pull the hairband from my long, dark ponytail, and take out my phone. I pretend to look at it as I walk past your table. In reality, the camera is taking a string of silent photos, including the page of notes you're working on. I let my favorite pen clatter to the ground next to you as I walk past. You stop writing.

"Hey, I think you dropped something," I hear behind me.

You lean down to pick it up, then walk over to return it to me. What a gentleman.

"Oh, thanks," I say, flipping my hair off my shoulder, acting the part of a flirtatious stranger.

I beam up at you, and you flicker a little self-conscious grin. I think I might see a hint of recognition in your expression, but you seem to shake it off when you realize you can't place my face. I'm sure you've seen me before, but

I am far too subtle for you to actually have figured out who I am.

"Well." I wink. "See you around."

You respond with a curious smile and a little wave. I saunter out of the café without looking back.

As soon as I turn the corner, I stop to jot down everything I can remember from our short interaction. The soft intensity of your gaze, the tone of your voice, my thoughts on the details you noticed about the strangers in your notes.

As I walk back to my apartment, a ridiculous pang of guilt strikes my conscience. It feels like it should be illegal, watching you this way. *Stalking* you. But all's fair in love and authorship, right? If you were a *real* person, my behavior would be terribly problematic. But fabricating these little interactions—writing myself into your scenes— has always felt like the best way to get to know you.

You think you have a standard life. You think you are average, even boring. But allow me to shed some light and say, this is not how you seem to me at all. As your author, I think I should have some authority on the subject.

In fact, you are my *favorite* character.

Where Light Shines
by Anne J. Hill

Awake in the shadows
The Darkness is lurking

Waiting for some poor soul
To stumble in the night.

A traveler approaches
The Darkness rejoices

Until it sees a lantern
With a flickering light

Disappointed, the Dark
Sulks away in the night

The Dark is forbidden
To go where light shines

The Ghost in the Thicket

by Emily Barnett

I t is unsettling to be so vulnerable and then realize, quite terribly, that you are not alone.

Willa rips off her tangled sheets and sits up, eyes roaming over the dark lumps and shadows of her room. Though all is still, her heart races because someone had whispered her name.

Instead of letting fear paralyze her, Willa tiptoes down the creaky stairs.

In the kitchen, her breath catches. A pair of gleaming eyes shine from atop the woodstove. A flash of terror clamors in her chest until she realizes that it's only Gus, their house cat, staring with disinterest.

Willa.

The voice. Her head snaps to the window. It reminds her of a train's distant whistle from miles away.

Come, it says.

Willa knows she shouldn't. It's the middle of the night.

Her parents will be worried if they wake up and find her missing. And the stories. There have been many strange happenings in the trees surrounding their farm. She had begged her grandpa to tell her the stories as a little girl, and they have haunted her ever since.

She knows she shouldn't. It isn't safe. But that voice—

Come, it says again with urgency, like someone caught in a well, their call distorted by stone and water and things hidden deep in the dark earth.

Like a ghost in white cotton, Willa slips from the back door and flies across the dew-laden grass, up over the moonlit moors, and through the heather that has taken on a blue hue. Every blade grasps her legs like sharp fingers, threatening to pull her under. The wind joins its cause as it sweeps through the meadow, tearing her hair and clawing her clothes. Willa tucks her head and runs faster, unsure if the night is driving her into the woods or trying to keep her out.

She pauses at the edge of the tangled shrubs and small trees. Not truly a forest, but merely a thicket, her dad would say. But he has never stepped foot inside. No one has in years.

But the one who beckons is there, hidden beneath its boughs.

Before she can talk herself out of it, Willa sucks in an icy breath and slips into the dense thicket.

And is swallowed.

The wind has stopped completely. Goosebumps crawl up her arms while the trees whisper down her neck. The ground is spongy and warm, as if the moss is too thick to be bothered with the cold earth far beneath. Willa turns back, but the opening is no longer there. The thicket is now a wood that has grown and stretched across the moors—devouring the land. Her eyes widen.

She will never get out.

Her grandfather's stories come quickly to the surface, and she tries in desperation to push them away. But they do not listen.

"There was said to be a ghost in the thicket." His coarse voice floated from her memories. "She haunted the woods at night, finding those who had lost their way."

"What did she do to them?" Willa had asked from the safety of his lap. "Did she *eat them?*"

But he never told her. He had only sighed and stared out the window, a glimmer in his eye. Then, he'd continued with other stories—about odd creatures and people who would sometimes stumble out of the thicket, as if they'd been chucked from a train and landed in a place they didn't recognize.

"Stay far from the thicket, Willa," he always said at the

end of his stories. "It is no place to wander."

A crow caws, triggering Willa back to the present.

Knowing she'll never get out if she gives into fear, Willa draws a deep breath and takes in her surroundings. There must be a plausible explanation.

But when she peers through the treetops, she gasps. The full moon from moments ago has been cleaved in half. Not only that, but the stars burn too bright—too warm. The leaves and bark in the wood are not painted in silvery blue but are washed in gold, like candles that do not flicker or go out.

A small whimper from behind slices through her. Staggering, she turns to the sound. A figure is retreating down a path. It is a boy, much younger than she. She hesitates. What if he is a ghoul? A demon? A trick of her imagination?

But what if he isn't, and he needs help?

Willa takes off down the winding trail, her nightgown snagging on branches. Following his sniffling, she comes around a bend and catches sight of him huddled on a log. The boy turns to flee again, but trips, sprawling onto the forest floor.

"Don't hurt me!" His small voice is muffled behind his arms. The boy's clothes are vintage: a button-down shirt, slacks pulled up to his ribs with suspenders and old work boots. He looks no older than nine. And he is trembling.

"I won't hurt you," Willa says. "I'm...lost."

When she takes two tentative steps closer, she bites back a scream. He is there, but not fully. A vapor. A mist. She had assumed the strange forest light had been playing tricks on her, but no. She'd been following a—

"Are-are you a ghost?" The boy's voice breaks.

Willa frowns. "Of course not," she says. "Aren't you?"

The boy straightens and wipes his eyes. The light around her pulses, and when she glances upward, the moon is now only a quarter. The candle-like glow around them shifts to something more akin to the nights she knows. But all the while, the boy's skin stays fluid, as if he is made of smoke.

"I'm Billy." He wipes his nose on a sleeve. "I'm lost too."

"How long have you been here?"

"Two days," he says, his face falling. "Do you know the way out?"

"No," she says, softening. "But we can look together."

The boy hesitates, clearly skeptical, but then his stomach grumbles, which Willa thinks is odd for a ghost.

"All right."

As they walk on the spongy moss, she glances back at the boy from time to time, trying to think of what to say, but when his dark eyes meet hers, she drops her gaze. He must be a phantom, lost between her world and the next. But how can she explain such a horrible thing to a child?

A breeze picks up and she shivers, crossing her bare arms once more. Why did she leave so hastily, without a coat or shoes? But then she remembers that strange voice pulling her onward. It was not the voice of the boy. Something more powerful had whisked her away. But was it friend or foe? Why did it not speak now?

A snapping stick causes them to stiffen. The boy grabs her hand. It is like ice, and she gasps, yanking away. His hurt expression quickly turns to trepidation as the cracking grows nearer. Heavy footfalls. Coming closer.

Closer.

Willa holds her breath, knowing running will only lead them deeper into the unknown.

Massive antlers split the darkness in front of them as a deer the size of a moose steps into the moonlight. Its pupils dilate as the beast snorts and breathes them in. Willa doesn't move an inch, even when the boy grabs her hand again.

It is no monster, but it's also no creature she has ever seen before. It eyes them warily at first, but then a lazy expression passes over its face, as if they are nothing but field mice. Turning, it crosses the path and trudges on.

"That...that was an Irish Elk," the boy whispers in awe.

"I studied them with Ma."

"I've never seen one before."

The boy looks at her with a funny expression. "No one has. They've been extinct for thousands of years."

She wrinkles her brow. *That's impossible. Ridiculous. He must be mistaken.*

But a trickle of cold runs down her back like a lone raindrop, the eerie touch of truth. An Irish Elk, the expanding woods, the changing moon and stars. It all feels archaic, yet somehow magically untainted by the years, as if she stands in a pocket outside of time. Or perhaps *in* time, just not hers. But what of Billy? She turns sharply to the boy.

"Billy, what year is it?"

"What do you mean? It's 1949."

She closes her eyes and swallows hard. Poor kid, haunting these woods for seventy years. She is grateful it has only felt like two days for him. Hopefully, that will always be the case. Unless she can get him out.

"Okay, Billy. Let's go."

With renewed vigor, she leads them back the way they'd come.

These bewitched trees can't last forever.

When she glances behind them, their feet leave no prints in the moss. They round a bend and see a small pool of water that hadn't been there before.

"I'm thirsty," Billy says, and crouches like a cat, lapping

water from his hands.

She almost tells him to be careful, but what can hurt someone already dead? She leans down beside him and stares into the pure water. The stars' brilliance cuts deep into the pond, lighting the rocky bed, and giant fish stirring beneath the calm surface. Before she can wonder if the fish are from her time or another, her eye catches on her reflection. The stars appear to be shining through her.

She touches her cheek, making sure it is no illusion, but is distracted by her hand. It is hazy, blurred.

She is smoke.

"Billy." Willa swallows, facing him. "Do...I...look like a ghost?"

Billy sits up from lapping the water and tips his head up. "Yep."

Trembling, she scrubs at her arms as if it will bring back its flesh. It can't be true. She would have remembered dying. She would have felt pain. Would have—

Had the voice been otherworldly? Ushering her into death. Calling her to the beyond.

Willa sucks in deep breaths of decomposing leaves and fresh earth. This is not what she imagined. What if she is eternally lost like Billy, in a forest stuck in time, with smoke for skin?

What if she has been lost for a year instead of a night?

She takes Billy's hand and lifts it to his face. "What do you see?"

He lifts his eyebrows. "My hand."

Willa shakes her head, then begins walking down the path again. Billy runs to catch up. She almost asks him about his past, but then stops herself. For some reason, it seems he can't see the truth of what he is—what he has become. Perhaps it is a curse. Or a grace. Either way, she won't be the one to tell him. Not when he is already so afraid.

Willa walks for so long and far that she nearly gives up. She would have, if not for the boy. Just as the moon changes for the fifth time, and the air around them glitters with silver, they come to an area that looks familiar.

Come, the voice beckons once more. Willa gasps. But this time the voice is warm; almost familiar. And as instinctively as she knows her mother's tone, she knows that the one who calls now, is ushering her home.

Just on the other side of the trees is their freedom. She glances back at the boy. What will happen when they leave? Will their souls be swept up to Heaven? Will they get a second chance at living? The thought is too much, and before she can dwell on the implications, she grabs Billy's hand and tugs him through behind her.

The sunlight is so shocking they both cry out in alarm.

But they are out. She blinks rapidly, looking down at

Billy. He is no longer hazy. He is whole. Relief and laughter bubble from them both.

"I'm home!" Billy yells, pointing toward her house. There is a small cut on his forehead and his face is pallid. A normal boy in the normal sun.

Willa looks down at her hands and her breath catches. They are still ghostly.

"I—I don't understand," she whispers.

"That's my house over there."

Willa cocks her head, momentarily distracted by his statement. She looks at the boy again.

"What's your full name?"

"William Davison. But I like Billy."

She smiles warmly. "I'm glad to have met you, Billy."

"Goodbye!" he yells, clearly thrilled to have made it home, no longer intrigued by a girl made of smoke.

The girl watches the boy crest the last hill and then run to his home. The door opens, and he is gathered up in the arms of a man and woman.

Willa looks down. Her feet make no indents in the tall grass. In fact, she hardly feels anything at all besides tired and numb. And grateful. If she couldn't have made it out alive, she was glad *he* did.

She lays down in the swaying heather and sleep quickly finds her.

"Willa?"

She stirs awake, her hair tangled around her. For a moment she thinks it's the voice that called to her before, but then a dark silhouette blocks out the sun and she squints up at a man.

"Are you Willa?"

"Yes." Her throat is dry and scratchy. Her stomach grumbles.

"We've been looking *everywhere* for you."

She tries to stand, but the world sways under her. The man gathers her up like a babe and hurries toward her home.

"I thought you'd never wake up," Willa's mother says, worry lining her eyes. "Where have you *been*?"

"How long was I gone?"

"Four days."

Willa breathes in her small room. She glances at her arms and smiles when her pillow gives way. She is alive. Solid. Not a ghost. Had it been a dream? If it had, where had she been all this time? And the boy...

Willa sits up.

"Mom, can you hand me that book?" She points to a very worn copy of *The Pocket of Time* that always sits on her nightstand. Her mother sighs, clearly frustrated that Willa hasn't answered any of her questions but gives into her request anyway.

"We had the cops looking for you. And the FBI. Even search dogs—" Her mother's voice cuts off. "What is it? What do you want with your grandfather's old book?"

Willa rubs her hand over the worn yellow cover. It reminds her of the stars' candle-like glow in the forest. Her fingers find the name *William Davison,* and she swallows hard.

"Just to remember," Willa whispers.

Willa flips open the cover that is falling apart and finds the dedication on the first page. She always wondered what it meant. Until now.

Her chest tightens as she reads.

To the ghost in the thicket, the girl of starlight and smoke, thank you for lighting my path. You found me just in time.
-Billy

Existence

by Denica McCall

I was born into a truth already existing
I am breathing with eternal lungs

Look what I've done
For you
Small babe, just
Opening those orbs of wonder to a wide world that seems
So much bigger than your fragile frame
And yet
Infinite things run through your veins
Whispers of what's next and
Endless potential

I saw what you gave, and
Wanted to give back, to make you proud, to
Prove to the onlookers that
I was meant to be here, that

Denica McCall

I can do this
So I fought and I raged against
The cage of the world's way, like
A prisoner of war, forgetting her
Origin
Bruised and battered by
Thoughts and lies draped with sincerity
Honestly, I
Felt I was doing the right thing, but then
This tick, this incessant critic kept tearing down
My joy, my
Persistence

Why aren't you there yet?
It taunted
There's still something wrong, you're
Singing the wrong song, and
Somehow you still don't belong

I was born into a throng of
Well-wishers and grave-diggers, a universe of
Beauty and pain all rolled into one ball of
Longing for its true name
And I knew it
Deep, deep inside where no one could see

Existence

I thought it was only me

And you,
You say I gave you something, I
Was enough, am enough, that I
Didn't take a wrong turn or
Fail at navigating the mysteries of my worth
That I'm
Not bad at praying or giving or loving

I was born into your grace,
Surrounded, even as an idea before I
Had a face or a place in this world
Before parents, before demons and powers
Your love was truth, and
Even now
Even now (I close my eyes in this moment,
Take a breath, feel it)
You say you want to do right by me, to
Show me your love
Despite the fact you've proven enough
Every breath
Every breath
Is you
And those infinite notions

That swim through the lines in my skin
And the pulse within,
I'm back at the beginning where
Existence is everything

Fading Out

by Natalie Noel Truitt

Ember is something that burns bright in the middle of something that is dying, fading out, soon to be nothing left.

One night, a girl steps onto an empty train with an unshakable feeling in her stomach that she won't be getting off at her stop.

When the train doors close and her world goes black, she knows she isn't alone, which is the most comforting, yet sometimes, the most desperate feeling in the world.

The loneliness she has felt for too long is so overwhelming that the presence of another being is suffocating.

Breaking. Broken. Gone. Dark.

"*What do you see?*" a voice asks from the other side of the train, or maybe it's right beside her, or worse, in her head.

She can't see anything.

But she can feel everything.

It's in that moment, in complete darkness, that she is engulfed by everything she is and everything she was made to be.

Sitting on the train, she is paralyzed. Paralyzed by lost opportunities and wrong words spoken. Paralyzed by being stuck in a career and in a life that is not everything she hoped it'd turn out to be.

"*What is your name?*" it asks.

And she does not know. She had once begged not to be alone, but now that she has this company, the very fibers that held her together become knitted with confusion in a way she could not even remember her own name.

She could only answer to this controlling force.

The power of the emotions spinning around her made her hold her hands over her ears and scream.

Scream for it to stop. The train to stop, her mind to stop, the darkness to lift.

Breaking. Broken. Gone. Dark.

Lost.

She is lost.

The entity follows her around wherever she goes on the train, but she is not sure that she has even moved an inch.

"*What do you see?*" it taunts. "*What is your name?*"

She does not know.

It claws at her mind like a billowing cloud that whispers a forgotten trace of a name she once knew. She knows she is different from before, but she doesn't know how.

She knows everything has changed, but she doesn't know why. Can a shadow of a girl spend a lifetime trying to remember herself while trying to forget everything else?

"I want out of this!" she cries into the nothingness.

Lost. Dark. Gone. Broken. Breaking. Nothing left. Fading out.

In the middle of something that is dying, something burns bright.

"Ember," a new voice whispers, "open your eyes." And she does.

The train doors open, and she sees a man standing there. "Come into the light?" He offers with an outstretched hand.

She steps off the train. The doors close behind her with a soft click, and she looks up at His face. "I don't want to ever go back there."

"You don't have to," He answers.

Ember is someone that burns bright in the middle of something that is dying.

And as the train pulls away, she is surrounded by light.

Light
by AJ Skelly

The darkness shrouds me

The night closes in

Blackness seeks me

Drags me under

Thrashing, wailing, tearing, staining

Everything is darkness

One pinprick

One tiny speck

There

AJ Skelly

It's rooted

Taken hold

It grows

It spreads

It battles the darkness within me

Thrashing, wailing, tearing, staining

The Light fights back

The Light gains ground

The world is dark

But the Light will not falter

It will not back down

The Light will save me

Hope in the Light

Light

Trust in the Light

The Light of life

Nightfall
by D.A. Randall

Sarita woke slowly, feeling heat and soreness all over her body. She blinked a few times against the bright sunlight, inhaling salty air. Lying on her side, she stared out at the open sea, rising and falling before her. Nothing but water, stretching for miles, in dark shades of blue beneath chill winds and feathery clouds. Her head lay on something soft and squishy. She half-rose to stretch out her aches.

She was seated on the edge of a dirty inflatable life raft. A hint of smoke permeated the air, irritating her nostrils.

She remembered now. The late-night party on the cruise ship. The explosion. The passengers running in all directions, screaming. A man in a tuxedo, his back on fire, jumping overboard to put out the blaze. Popping flames roaring throughout the ship like they had all been placed in the center of a crackling fire pit.

Sarita blinked a few more times, rousing herself, and

turned to view the rest of her boat.

On the opposite end, a few feet away, a quiet man sat staring at her, his head entirely bandaged, his eyes hidden by sunglasses like the Invisible Man.

Sarita screamed and scrambled backward.

The bandaged man jerked in his seat, startled, causing the boat to tip from side to side like a seesaw. Sarita stopped herself, irritated at her childish outburst. She gripped the sides of the raft and forced her nerves to calm, as the bandaged man did the same. They sat motionless, waiting for the boat to settle. The man held up a gloved hand, motioning her to remain still.

"I apologize," Sarita said. "I was just surprised, that's all. I thought I was alone." She glanced down at herself. Thank God she had chosen to wear a pantsuit to the gala instead of a dress. The satin was torn at the sleeve and over one thigh, and her heeled shoes sat on the soft floor before her feet, where three toes poked through a stocking. But her clothes could be replaced. She was lucky to be alive.

She examined the man sharing her lifeboat. He was trim and oddly dressed in a long-sleeved jacket and pants, with sneakers and thin leather gloves. Obviously not a corporate party guest or even one of the ship's waiters. He also seemed strangely calm, for having just survived an explosion on a crowded ship. Yet he jerked at the cry of a passing seagull. Perhaps, beneath his quiet exterior, he felt as nervous as she did. Perhaps more so.

She turned to her left, where smoke rose from the water in the distance. They had nothing left to return to.

"Do you know what happened?" she asked. "How long have we been here? I remember something exploded on the ship and everyone started running. Someone in the crowd knocked against me, and I fell."

The man nodded, but pointed to his throat and shook his head.

Sarita stiffened. "I'm sorry. You can't speak?"

He shook his head again. Pointing to Sarita, he raised both his hands and angled his body forward as if he was falling. Then he pointed to himself.

"Is that sign language?"

He shook his head again. The man was mute, but not deaf. Perhaps whatever caused his silence had happened recently.

"You saw me fall?" Sarita asked.

He nodded, pointing to himself and Sarita, making a motion of cradling a baby in his arms. He spread his arms out over the raft.

"You brought me here," she said.

Another nod.

"Thank you. What happened to the ship? The Board

of Directors. We were about to–"

The bandaged man shook his head. He crossed his hands, forming an X, then spread them apart, as if shoving a pile of dry leaves out of his way. She understood clearly.

No more.

She glanced back at the distant plume of smoke, and imagined her co-workers being consumed by an enormous blaze and turned to ash. "Everyone in the firm?" she asked. "The whole ship?" Sarita felt her lip quivering and tried to stifle it as the man looked away, studying the sea in mournful silence. Her shoulders trembled in the breeze. The two of them were alone, adrift at sea with no one around for miles. She inhaled deeply, releasing it slowly. The worst thing they could do now was to panic. She regarded the bandaged man. "Thank you for saving me," she said. "I'm Sarita Castillo. What's your name?"

The man cocked his head to one side, looking apologetic.

"I'm sorry," she said. "You can't tell me. Do you mind if I give you a name? Then I don't have to keep saying, 'Hey, you.' Why don't I call you Knight, since you're the white knight who rescued me?"

The man paused, then allowed a small shrug.

Her eyes searched the floor of the raft. She shifted to look behind herself. "Did you see a small purse I had with me?"

Knight shook his head.

"Probably dropped it when everyone ran," she said with a sigh. "I don't suppose you have a cell phone?" She scanned every direction of the open sea as he shook his head again. There were no ships in sight, only the smoking remains of the one they had escaped from. "Not that we could expect to get service out here, anyway. Any flare guns on board?"

Again, no.

She tightened her lips. "So we just have to wait. It's only a matter of time before we're spotted by a passing boat or a helicopter or something. Can you tell me what you were doing on the ship?"

Knight glanced away, as if reluctant to answer. Then he raised his finger to trace a letter "Z" in the air.

"You're with Zeherquist Domain?" Sarita asked. "You work for them?"

Knight cocked his head slightly, then shook it.

"But you're involved with them somehow?"

He nodded, looking away again.

"My firm was there to consider supporting their work," Sarita said. "But we found some of their projects a bit questionable, to say the least. They told us they were making advances in medical treatments. But our research team found intel that suggested they were conducting unsanctioned biological experiments. They seem bent on creating various sorts of weaponized soldiers-for-hire. Sound about right?"

Knight's chest swelled and released slowly. He gave a solemn nod.

"If that explosion was their fault, we'll demand a full investigation. And however you're involved in it, you'd better–"

Knight shook his head vigorously.

Sarita paused. "No company loyalty?" she asked.

He shook his head with a definite "no."

Sarita sighed. "Well, that makes it easier for us to work together, I suppose. Any idea what caused the explosion?"

No.

"But you think Zeherquist Domain was responsible?"

Yes.

"Then we'll deal with them later. For now, we'll watch for a passing ship. Hopefully, we'll see someone, or better yet, they'll see us, before we get dehydrated. We just have to be patient until help arrives." She leaned back, assuming a relaxed position.

Knight rested his arm on the raft, following suit. He stared at the boat's rim beneath his arm.

And kept staring.

"What?" Sarita asked. "What is it?"

Knight squeezed the edge of the raft, trying to pinch part of it between his fingers.

"What's wrong?" Sarita whispered.

His chest swelled and retracted rapidly. He gripped the raft tightly, then held up his curled hand, as if it still rested on the rubber rim. He closed the resting hand slowly. Slowly.

Slowly.

Her eyes widened. She squeezed the firm raft as hard as she could and felt the slightest give.

They were sinking.

"We're losing air." She swallowed. "How long?"

He felt the side of the raft again and shrugged.

Sarita tightened her lips. "We'll run into someone eventually, in a day or two. We're not losing air that fast. I've driven on low tires that lasted for a few days, so–so we should be all right until someone finds us."

Knight continued to study the sea. Then shook his head slowly.

"Why not?"

He pointed far away to his left. Sarita turned. About fifty yards away, a fin poked out of the water, gliding smoothly along, just beneath the surface.

A pointed fin.

Sarita's lip trembled as it dipped back under the water and disappeared. "It probably won't hurt us. It's over there, minding its own business. It might not even be aware of us."

Knight continued to stare in the creature's direction. She looked back again.

And saw another shark fin farther away, swimming in the opposite direction.

She worked to steady her breathing. Hyperventilating wouldn't help either of them. They had to keep their heads. "Is that normal? Seeing two sharks at once? Something had to attract them, right?"

Yes.

"Is it us?"

No.

"Aren't they attracted to blood in the water? There would have to be some kind of–" She gasped. "The ship. The explosion. We haven't drifted that far from it."

Knight nodded.

She licked her lips. "But they'll swim to the ship. The dead bodies there. They'll leave us alone."

Knight made no response.

Sarita didn't see much hope in it, either, as her breath came out in quick gasps. She timed her breathing, like a woman in labor, keeping herself in control. "What about the ship? There must be something there we can use.

Perhaps another life raft. Or some debris we can use to stay afloat. Or to drive the sharks away."

He faced her and tapped his wrist, as if referring to a watch. Shielding his eyes, he pointed upward at the sun, then down.

"Time?" she asked. "When the sun goes down. Nightfall. That's how long we have?"

Yes.

"Why? The raft should last through the night. We just have to hold out until we're spotted."

He shook his head and pointed back at the sea where the sharks had appeared. As if on cue, a third fin broke the distant surface.

Sarita swallowed. "They hunt at night," she said, her throat feeling strangled.

The bandaged man gave another slow nod, like a death knell.

Nightfall.

They had until nightfall.

The hours passed slowly. Tediously. They watched the sea and the sky for any passing boat or plane, but saw nothing all afternoon. They also watched the ocean's surface, broken by the occasional shark fin. Fins that appeared closer to them every hour, by Sarita's estimation. "Knight, can I ask what happened to you?"

Knight stared at the raft floor. Instead of answering, he felt the side of the raft again, staring at the section he had squeezed.

Sarita didn't want to know how much air they had lost.

He lifted his head and shrugged, drawing a "Z" in the air again.

"Zeherquist Domain," she said. "They're responsible for your injuries?"

Yes.

"They experimented on you, didn't they? You're one of the people they were trying to weaponize."

Yes.

"Are you all right?" she asked. "If we–*when* we get back–we can find you a hospital. Some treatment."

He regarded the smoking remains of the cruise ship. Then stared in the opposite direction at the endless sea.

"There must be something that doctors can do to help you," Sarita offered.

No.

"But surely someone can–"

His hand sliced through the air, ordering her to silence with a sudden rage.

She gripped the sides of the deflating raft, holding her breath. "All right," she said. "I'm sorry. I'm only trying to help."

He returned to his study of the empty ocean, his fist clenching the side of the raft.

Then he gripped his forehead so suddenly she feared he was about to rip away his bandages. He looked as though he wanted to tear his own skin off. Zeherquist Domain had done something horrible to him, in their quest to create human weapons. Whatever their experiments involved, it had damaged his mind as well as his body.

She was clinging to life in a sinking boat with a madman.

Nightfall.

The sharks had drawn closer. Sarita caught glimpses of the large fins in the flashes of moonlight. Her entire body tensed, staring at the black sea of death.

Then she saw it. A tiny light, beyond the area where the cruise ship had gone down, its smoke having dissipated earlier. Someone must have seen or heard about the explosion and finally sent someone to investigate.

"We're saved!" she pointed. "Look! We're saved!"

He looked in the direction she indicated. Past the cruise ship that he had refused to acknowledge all afternoon. He studied it for a while before shaking his head.

"What do you mean?" Sarita demanded. "They're right there. Probably searching for the ship."

He pointed down at their raft, then at the distant passing lights. He pressed his hands together, then spread them apart as far as he could.

"You're saying they're too far? They won't see us?"

He gave a firm nod, then raised a finger.

"But what?" she asked.

He pointed at her and made a circling motion.

She waited for more. "I don't understand. What needs to turn in a circle?"

He pointed at her.

"You...want me to turn around?"

He nodded.

"Why?" she asked. "No, there's no reason for me to do that."

He circled again with his finger.

"No!" she said. "That won't help us. Whatever needs to be done, we can do it together. We have to trust each other or we'll never make it."

He shook his head with the same violence he had displayed earlier, as if he might lash out at her any second.

He twirled his finger again. He meant to throw her overboard. To lighten the load and keep himself afloat long enough to be rescued, once her back was turned.

She shook her head. "No. Please. We can figure this out."

A fin broke the water beside them about twenty feet away. Sarita shrieked. She had no way to escape. She couldn't fight the bandaged man, and any attempt to stop him might toss them both into the deep.

Knight pointed sharply at her, then spun his finger hard, as if barking a command for her to face the dead black sea.

Sarita shook her head again, trembling.

He lunged forward suddenly and seized her shoulders. He forced her to turn and look over her edge of the raft.

"No, please!" she cried. She tried to wriggle free of his grip, but the raft shook like a boat in a tiny storm, drawing water into its center. He clutched her forearms, squeezing hard to hold her in place. She obeyed and kept still, gasping as a shark fin passed fifteen feet ahead. Resisting him would only kill them both.

The night winds chilled her quivering shoulders. She sat on her knees and waited breathlessly.

She heard him unzip his jacket.

"What are you doing?"

He lunged forward again, shaking the boat as his gloved hand pressed against her cheek, guiding her to look straight ahead. She obeyed as he continued to remove his jacket behind her.

"If you're planning to swim, you'll never make it. And if you're casting off weight, just–just don't do anything you'll regret. You'll have to live with your decision, for the rest of your life."

He ignored her. She heard the jacket drop onto the rubber floor between them as another fin rippled the water, only ten feet away.

She turned toward the lights. "Look. The ship's not that far away. They'll reach us soon."

He grabbed her temples and forced her head painfully away from the ship, back toward the open sea. He was insane and unpredictable. All she could do was hope for the other ship to get there faster. *Faster!*

"Please," she begged. "Please, for *God's sake!*"

He touched her back, making her flinch. Then his arm jutted straight past her face, pointing at the open sea.

"All right," she said. "I won't turn. Just, please. I won't tell anyone what happened. You haven't done anything wrong yet. It was Zeherquist Domain. What they did to you. You're not thinking straight."

Knight did not respond as Sarita sat on her knees in the

puddle that had splashed into the raft. A thin layer of water now coated the entire rubber floor, as another shark passed six feet before her eyes.

They were sinking faster, as the angular fins continued to cut through the waves around them. Their struggles had drawn in too much water. Now they were minutes away from plunging into the deep, right into the circle of sharks.

Sarita shook and found herself whimpering. They were drowning in a dark sea, and would be eaten alive before they ran out of air. The ship's last survivor, her only hope of escape, was insane or a murderer or both. She couldn't help crying. This was madness. No one should die like this. *No one!*

She wanted to check on the ship, to see how close it was. But doing so would only enrage Knight all the more, and perhaps send them both into the sharks' waiting mouths.

She strained to listen for what he was doing, as she saw two fins at once, drawing closer. It sounded as though he was peeling apart fabric, over and over.

He was removing his bandages.

What was wrong with him? Did he want to show her how badly they had damaged him?

She heard some other fabric slipping off. One, then the other. His gloves?

Then she noticed the light. The dark sea had become

lighter.

She started to turn, but Knight jumped at her again, pushing her face toward the sea of circling sharks.

With a hand that glowed like a blinding beacon.

She stared ahead at the shark fins that had become clearer, as though a spotlight now shone on them. She heard the sunglasses fold together behind her. The light spread and intensified, and the sharks began to submerge in retreat. She heard the shirt pulling away from his skin, and then the entire ocean – the entire *world* – lit up like daybreak.

Tears continued to stream down her cheeks, but they had changed from tears of horror to tears of joy. They were saved. Saved by a freak accident that had turned this poor mute man into a human beacon, one that could be seen across miles and miles of ocean. He wasn't waiting for nightfall to throw her to the sharks. He was waiting for nightfall so that he could remove his bandages and shine in every direction. With a light so intense that staring at it might blind her.

Sarita wiped at her cheeks, starting to laugh as she kept her body turned away from Knight, knowing the distant ship would veer toward them as the sharks continued to depart. She realized how true it was, the old saying...

It's always darkest before the dawn.

A Taste of Life
by Beka Gremikova

*T**his is a bad idea.*
Tristan stood on the edge of the forest, clutching a box of croissants to his chest. He sucked in a deep breath. Intruding upon the wraiths that dwelt here did not appeal to him. *Surely food is the way to the heart, even for vengeful ghosts.*

If he was wrong... He shuddered at the thought, staring around at the dark, towering trees. He'd heard from others who'd attempted to visit dead loved ones that if the wrong Flickers caught him before daybreak, he'd be dead.

Tristan swiveled on his heels, searching out the comforting lights of the village in the distance.

I should go back.

But Aimée's face hovered in his mind, the way he'd so often seen it over the years: bright smile, eyes crinkling at the corners, messy curls floating around her cheeks.

He needed to make things right with her, even if it

killed him.

He glanced down doubtfully at the box of croissants. In life, Aimée had always loved them. But would she care for them still after the way she'd died?

Don't do it, a voice in his head warned. *You'll regret it. If you get into trouble, only a Victim's Right can save you!*

The Victim's Right, handed down by the Creator, gave the wronged person the power to decide the fate of their afflicter. It had been a part of their country's justice system for centuries, and to deny a Victim's Right risked grave consequences.

And if Tristan had wronged anyone, it was undoubtedly Aimée.

He squared his shoulders and turned back toward the woods, marching along the path through the trees. Aimée deserved better than his fear. And by the spirits! He needed some closure, some sort of peace.

With shaking hands, Tristan opened the box, seeking strength for the night ahead. He picked up a croissant, and after a moment's hesitation, nibbled at it. The soft freshness of butter melted on his tongue, then the sharp kick of strong, aged cheese.

He closed his eyes, memories flooding his mind. Aimée bringing him to her favorite bakery. Sitting outside in the sunshine, enjoying pastries and discussing the latest fashions. Aimée, wane and sickly pale, limbs twitching, suffering from the Dancing Plague that caused its victims to dance themselves to death. His parents, begging him to give her up to save his own life.

He stared down at the croissant he held. The plague had begun due to spoiled flour, but barely six months later, the bakeries were flourishing once again.

He straightened. He didn't want Aimée's last experience of her favorite sweet to be tainted.

He snuck another croissant, its light, warm taste as comforting as a kiss. The feeling carried him forward, deeper into the darkness of the forest.

Nestled within the heart of the woods lay the cemetery. Moonlight illuminated the now-open graves of the Dancing Plague victims. Only one Flicker lingered, running ghostly fingers over the inscription engraved into her tombstone: *Rest in better peace and enjoy an eternal feast.*

Tristan recognized that thin, willowy figure. Heart racing, he whispered, "Aimée?"

She whirled, her wild black hair melding into the darkness, her skin gleaming like a will-o'-the-wisp. White flames flickered in her eyes.

"Tristan!" Her voice was an eerie echo. She floated toward him, head tilted.

He took a few steps backward, unsure of her reaction.

Would she attack him, as other Flickers seemed to do when they came across one of the living?

He bumped against a tree trunk.

"Why do you look like I'm going to eat your heart for breakfast?" Aimée crossed her arms, eyes narrowed at him.

"Y-you know what Flickers do to people!" he sputtered. "Maiming is one of their favorite pastimes!"

The white flames in her eyes died a little. She sighed. "Not all of us," she murmured. "Some of us believe Death is too long to spend in hatred."

Heat rushed into his cheeks. He was doing this whole bittersweet-reunion-for-the-sake-of-peace thing very, very badly. He rubbed his eyes. "I'm sorry, Aimée. For...everything."

"That's an extremely vague term." Despite the thin quality of her voice, it held all the sharpness it had boasted in life.

He swallowed. "I shouldn't have left you..." He trailed off as Aimée's eyes landed on the box in his hands.

"What's that?" she demanded.

His heart pounded harder in his chest. Around them, the trees shivered under a gust of wind. Hesitantly, he cracked open the lid. "Maybe I shouldn't have brought these. I don't even know if you *can* eat."

She peered inside, and her chin snapped up. Her eyes

blazed, and Tristan's heart nearly stopped.

"What in the name of the Plague were you *thinking*?" she hissed. She reached out, her hands turning to flesh as she snatched the box away from him. "Croissants? The things that *killed* me? You have the audacity to bring my murder weapon to my grave!" Her skirt whipped around her legs, and Tristan suddenly feared tomorrow's headlines would read: Cause of Death: BAKED GOODS BASHED INTO SKULL.

He threw up his hands. "Aimée, I didn't mean to offend—"

"What *did* you mean, then? I knew you had your moments, but *this*—" Her voice shook. "Are you trying to rub it in that I'm dead?"

"No!" he gasped. Oh, saints preserve him! Or maybe not. It'd be too much work to help him right now. "I— Aimée—that's the *last* thing I want to do!"

"Well, state your intentions, then!" she snapped. "Before I personally feed you to the other Flickers myself!"

Suddenly, his intentions seemed ludicrous. But that was all he had to offer. "I wanted to give you a better final taste of your favorite sweets. I wanted you to have the chance to enjoy it again, to laugh under the moonlight even if you can't see the sun." He flushed. He was no poet—that had been Aimée's talent. "I thought since some time had passed...maybe you *could* enjoy them?" With each word, he felt himself digging his own grave. He swallowed.

Yet the fire in her eyes dimmed, and she cracked open the lid wider, her nostrils flaring to catch that fresh-baked-bread aroma.

Was that drool in the corner of her mouth?

Aimée picked one of the croissants, holding it up for inspection. "Lovely crescent moon shape, flaky and light in texture." She paused in thought. "Perhaps... I spoke in haste. Only anger could drive me away from my darling croissants."

"You had me scared there for a moment." Tristan rubbed at his chest with a nervous chuckle. "I thought I was done for..." And that the girl he loved had lost *her* love for pastries. Still, he held his breath as she took a bite and chewed slowly, her lips pursed. Then the sweet, almost gleeful grin he knew so well stretched across her face.

"No matter how much I want to, I just can't hate these croissants." She shook her head. "That baker must be a witch—these taste even better than when I was alive!" She knelt across from him on the grass, the box on her lap. "Don't think this absolves you. I'm just hungry." She glanced at him. "But Tristan, I think you should leave before Lilette gets back..."

A shudder rolled down his spine. While alive, Lilette

had been well known for her pointed, angry tongue—and her hatred of sweets.

"Don't tell me—"

Aimée nodded. "If you thought *my* reaction was scary, hers will make you wish *I'd* killed you."

His throat closed. It was rather difficult, after hoping for resolution and a chance to talk things out, to be hurried on his way. "Might I stay just a few moments?"

"Well, don't say I didn't warn you."

"Believe me, I've been warning myself ever since I thought of coming here."

She rolled her eyes. "At least *one* side of your brain has survival instinct." She sighed, then dropped the box between them on the ground. "Well, while you're here, you can help me finish these before Lilette and the others show up."

"Where do they go?" He picked up a croissant, its flaky texture crumbling in his hand.

"Oh, you know, the usual. Scaring sleeping squirrels, harassing owls, floating spookily around cabins in the middle of the woods." She held up her croissant to him in a silent toast.

They bit into the rolls. That same delicious sharpness spread across his tongue, eating away at the last crumbs of fear coating his heart.

At first, Aimée gobbled hers down, peeking over her shoulder as though she expected her fellow Flickers to appear at any moment. But with each croissant, she relaxed even more until she almost looked like the Aimée he'd known: content, happy to chatter away over a hot coffee and croissant, whether in a café or in the middle of a graveyard.

"Aimée." He reached out but didn't dare to touch her. "I...I really am sorry for what I did. Leaving you, causing more hurt with these pastries... All of it."

She looked at him, and the pain and sorrow in her eyes felt like a punch to his chest. She picked up another croissant and tore off a piece, rubbing it between her fingers. "While I was dying, I hated you," she admitted. "But when I thought about how Papa would have to bury me, I understood why your parents asked you to end our courtship."

His eyes stung. "I wish I—"

"Wishing can't change anything. You can't wish away what you did—that doesn't make your apology any better." She bit her lip. "But braving this place to bring me a piece of my old life—no matter how misplaced your choice in food was—it shows me your true heart. Your ridiculous yet earnest soul." A smile flickered around her mouth. "And it's—"

"Aimée!" A chorus of outraged Flickers swept into the glade. Ragged white garments hung from their limbs, which twitched under the Plague's effects. Their blazing red eyes fixed on Tristan. At the front of the throng stood a woman with long, flowing white hair, her lips thin and twisted in rage.

Lilette.

She kicked at the box of croissants, sending them flying. "Did *you* bring these?" she hissed at Tristan.

"I—"

"How *dare* you! When we all died from eating blighted goods!"

Aimée stretched out her hands. "Lilette, this is a private matter. He brought them as a gift to *me*, not an affront to *you*."

"Nothing in this forest by night is a *private matter*. The graveyard is for the living by day and for the dead by night," Lilette said, spreading her arms wide.

"My intent—" Tristan began, his mind scrambling.

"Intentions mean nothing!" Lilette snapped. As one, she and the other Flickers surrounded Tristan, their voices raised in a loud, overwhelming chant. He strained to catch a glimpse of Aimée's wild black curls, but she'd disappeared in the swirl of silver and gossamer.

His heart thundered at the sight of all those piercing,

glittering smiles.

"I needed to make amends," he whispered.

"Oh, you shall. Just as we danced ourselves to death, you will, too." Grabbing his arms with spectral strength, Lilette and the other Flickers pulled him into a dance. He staggered to keep up with their undead speed and grace.

He caught a glimpse of Aimée, struggling to battle her way to him through the dancers. Her lips formed words, but the high, lilting song of the Flickers overwhelmed her voice. They pushed her back toward the edge of the clearing, far from where Tristan spun about in the middle of the horde, trapped in Lilette's arms.

Lilette and her ghostly dancers spun Tristan through the cemetery, dancing between life and death, around trees and tombstones, over and over...

His limbs shuddered. He felt gnawed, chewed and spat out. His own mortality tasted like stale bread and rotting cheese.

His chest heaved. He caught a fleeting glimpse of dark hair, and then his vision dimmed. His stomach twisted with another sickening twirl. He staggered—into Aimée's arms.

She threw back her head and shrieked, "Victim's Right!"

The Flickers froze in their dance, staring. A hiss slithered through them, and they retreated from Tristan, glowering at Aimée.

Tristan gasped for breath as Aimée guided him towards the safety of the trees with gentle, measured steps. The world slowly stopped spinning.

"The Right is meant to offer personal revenge!" Lilette's eyes blazed, and she clenched her fists. "You misused it!"

"We have very different ideas about the Right," Aimée said coldly, helping Tristan slump to the ground. "The Right is to offer closure and peace. I wish to let him live."

Lilette's eyes burned into Tristan as the first touch of dawn flushed her face. "You're a lucky man. We cannot interfere when the Right is claimed—but don't think this is an invitation to return." She and the other Flickers sank into their graves, and the cemetery grew quiet once more.

Tristan clutched at Aimée. "I...Aimée, thank you." His mind scrambled, but he couldn't think of anything to say that didn't sound trite, so instead, he pointed at the upturned box. "I think there's still one more, if you'd like," he whispered.

"Think I can eat it that fast?" she teased, her form growing more translucent as the sun strengthened.

His throat tightened, but he forced his tone to match hers. "I know you can."

She gave a soft, rippling laugh before snatching the last

croissant and taking a huge bite. "That taste," she hummed. "It makes me feel *almost* alive again." She reached out to touch his cheek. "You know...feel free to send a box now and then. I'll eat them in front of Lilette for entertainment." She winked and floated over to her grave. He averted his gaze, unable to watch her sink into the ground.

"Rest in peace, Tristan," he heard her murmur, and then daylight had taken over the clearing. But her words followed him home, and the first thing he did was visit the bakery, with a request for a box of croissants to be delivered to Aimée's grave every fortnight.

"After all," he said to the baker's son, who looked at him in horror, "food is the way to the heart—even for vengeful ghosts."

Hollow

by Denica McCall

Hollow dark
Threatens to steal the night's
Magic
Empty time is the weapon that wages
Against my mind
However, this canopy of truth
Reminds me of your words
I've got you, see
I've got you
You billow around me
You come down, surround, you
Fill my resounding question mark
Echoing inside this chest, your
Courage gives me rest
Your pain pounds on this breast
Deeper and deeper until I know
You know

Denica McCall

Light in these skies
Can't be concealed by
Formless shadows
Minds like to play tricks but
Truth is what sticks
You're my orchestra and I'm
The venue filled with lights and
Breath
Play to me now
So I can play to the rest

Out of the Sea
by Savannah Jezowski

I rise, out of the sea, I rise,
a specter of the deep,
salt-kissed skin and seaweed hair
and briny fish scales.
I hear the call of canvas sails
snapping wild in the wind,
the stir of oars dipping
in my bed of sea foam.
I see wild souls who do not heed
the warnings of the rocks
and plot their course across
the Siren's watery realm.

I sing a song of lost dreams,
of shadows reaching
across the barren seas
to taint the crest of waves

that kiss the barnacled hulls of ships.
I tantalize their senses
on fog-cloaked seas concealed
and draw them deftly to me;
they come, fools reaching for their deaths.
So I sing a song of passion,
of steel fishhooks
and sun-bleached mermaid bones.

Gently I banish their fears,
curl my mists around their eyes,
raise the ghosts of past ships
caught in my embrace.
Specters haunt the listing deck,
calling their brothers
to join them in my black waters
with the other skeletal ships.
I rise, out of the sea, I rise
to sing a sultry song
that beckons all the sailors
to the siren's watery grave.

I sing a song of hatred
with monsters from the deep;
my song strikes out like thunder

rolling across the waves.
I raise the ships with ghost shroud
to dance across the seas
as dry-lightning flashes
across the writhing sky.
I sing—terror fills their wild eyes
as their blood begins to freeze.
I drag the ships of sailors
to the fathoms of the deep.

I sing a song of loneliness,
The oceans still and barren,
the ships afraid to leave their moorings
and venture across my waves.
They snared my sisters,
I sank their ships,
but now what remains?
Only mermaid bones and lifeless sails
and memories of regret.
The seas are mine now.
I sink into the waves and wish
we'd chosen more than death.

I rise, out of the sea, I rise,
a specter bent on change,

Savannah Jezowski

gone the days of sinking ships
and battle tridents.
I hear the call of canvas sails
snapping once again,
and when the sailor falls
I fetch him from my waves.
I sing a song to reconcile
The realms that once waged war.
Can salty seas and salty tears
Mend the scars we've made?

The Guardian of the Maelstrom
by Maseeha Seedat

My father traveled the seas. His father traveled the seas, and so did his father before him. The men in my family have always traveled, searching the world for a legacy. They spent months away from home, and when they returned—which was seldom, for most of their voyages ended in disaster—they brought back wild, far-fetched legends that soon disappeared into the pages of fantasy.

That all ended when I was born.

My mother had never stepped foot out of our village. She was born there, raised there, and died there. It was my fault. She lost her life giving birth to me. But my father said she wasn't gone and that I reminded him of her every day. I never saw the resemblance. Maybe I chose not to, so I wouldn't have to face what caused my father to lose the light of his life.

He never remarried and never had a son. He sold our

house and raised me—a woman—on the open seas, with the sunsets, the wonders and mysteries of the deep, at the risk of his own reputation.

I learned to listen to the wind and navigate the stars. I mastered the art of knots and memorized the shanties belted out by the crew. I was the best deckhand on *Valka;* everyone knew it. But I never commanded the crew. That was for the men.

Our tiny band of explorers set sail from America, hoping to cross the Atlantic before winter arrived. This stirred a murmuring below deck, a dangerous whisper that dragged you in and never let you go. Rumors infected the crew as we wondered why my father had set three months for a voyage that took most ships two. But we dared not question him to his face. It was Captain's orders. My father had to know what he was doing.

"Isla!" he called from the helm. The sun had barely risen, glistening at the edge of the silent horizon. "Climb up to the nest."

I glanced at the first mate, Ray. He had known my father since they were children. He knew I hated the nest. Out here, in the middle of nowhere, the wind blew wildly, rocking the mast until it swayed like a drunken sailor. I silently pleaded with him to take my place. He shook his head sadly. Captain's orders. I had to obey.

"Aye, Captain!"

I scaled the mainmast's nets, following a path I knew from memory. My callused fingers barely noticed the gnarled rope or the chilled wind. It took no time to reach the top. I pulled myself into the wooden basket that peeked over the mainsail.

"What do you see?" my father hollered.

I raised the spyglass to my eye, blinking an image into focus. Storm clouds loomed over the southern horizon, thick and heavy, darker than the deepest depths of the ocean. They stood unwavering, waiting to set the waters in motion, to build waves towering over the biggest ships of men. Lightning flickered through their elegant curves, followed by the roaring thunder, a warning to stay away. A shimmering, grey sheet of rain hung between the clouds and the ocean. Gallons of frigid water pounded against the once-still surface of the Atlantic.

My father was headed right for the storm.

"Storm!" I yelled, praying he heard me as the clouds sent a howling gale toward *Valka*. I turned the spyglass to him, but I didn't need it to see the madness on his face or the terrifying gleam in his sea-green eyes. He knew the strength of a storm, the resolute violence it could hold, yet here he was, unwavering as the clouds, steering us straight toward it.

I jumped onto the lip of the crow's nest, hunched on all fours to stay balanced. Pulling the cutlass from my waist, I leaped into the air, and, for a moment, I saw everything. The world was still, even the clamoring birds as they fled the storm. There was nothing for miles, just blue. Blue sky, blue ocean, blue everything. I turned, and I saw the storm again, closer than before, a couple of miles away. A shout of thunder escaped the clouds, and my heart drummed faster in reply, battering against my ribs.

I hooked my sword—the one my father had gifted my mother years ago—over the rope, careening down to the stern. My leather gloves stopped the blade from cutting into my palm as I zipped down the line, whooping at the top of my lungs.

As I landed, the flat of my blade hit my father on the head. He staggered backward, losing grip of the wheel. It spun maniacally, and the ship veered hard left, knocking me off balance. Crates slid down the deck, slamming into the crew members struggling to stay on their feet. The rails dipped in the water as the current threatened to drown us.

I did the first thing my instincts told me to do: I grabbed the wheel.

As soon as my father found his feet, he wrenched the wheel out of my grasp, setting course for the storm again.

"You have one rule on this ship, Isla," he fumed, placing his hat back on his head. "Never touch the wheel. Never. Do you know how dangerous it is for a woman to be on board a ship, let alone be raised on one? I'm pushing my luck having you here at all without you trying to steer."

"Of course. I know how much is at stake. I know the downfall we face if I slip up. I know! I get it! All right? I only held the wheel for a second."

"And the only reason you did was because your sword knocked me on the head. Come on, hand it over." He held his palm out to me.

My hands fell to the hilt of my mother's blade. I lowered my head in shame. "I'm sorry, Captain. I won't touch the wheel again. I promise."

His face softened, and he placed a firm hand on my shoulder. "I know, but just to be safe..." His hand dropped from my shoulder to my wrist, pulling the sword out of my fingers. "You'll get it back at sunrise."

By now, the rest of the crew could see the storm, and the wave of dread was visible through their eyes. Every one of us shuddered at the slightest sign of an ocean storm. It brought fear, anger, desperation. In a storm, anything and everything could happen. Emotions bubbled at the surface;

tongues flicked like swords; hearts took control of the mind. In a storm, every barricade of common sense was swept aside by the gales. All that remained was pure, raw, undeniable truth.

"This is going to be rough, boys!" my father hollered over the winds. "Secure your lifelines! Fasten the cargo! Hands ready on the sails!"

We obeyed, and I raced to tie my rope around my waist.

Valka ducked under the curtain of rain.

This was the fifth storm I had faced in my life, and the one lesson that stuck with me through the first four was this: the best thing to do was to head for the shallowest waves and the lowest winds. My father did the exact opposite, his ego controlling his decisions. He was here searching for a legacy, and he wouldn't leave without finding it. He plowed the bow through wave after wave, each larger than the one before, his face lit with a manic glow. When the waves were too big, immovable hills of black water, we climbed, teetered on the pinnacle, and raced down the slopes to the other side.

The crew didn't complain. It was Captain's orders. My father knew what he was doing. He had to have some sort of plan hidden under his drenched tricorne.

The ocean was relentless, rolling on every side of us. Its

foaming breath lashed at the decks, tossing the sails like paper in a breeze. The waves closed around *Valka*, holding her firmly as they shoved her back and forth. The waters turned to the color of mud as the waves arched high over our heads. Winds shifted to gales, forcing us to reef the mainsail as the icy gusts seeped through our clothes, chilling us to the very core.

We must have faced fifty lethal waves before my father smiled. We were here.

Valka hung on for dear life as she slipped into the eye of the storm. Lightning flickered over our faces, illuminating our fear and awe. Legends had spoken of the eye of the storm, its silence, its beauty, its stillness. With the thunder roaring overhead, the water was silent.

My father had set our course straight for a maelstrom. A gyrating funnel that sucked ships in with no hope of escape. A black hole with secrets as enchanting as a siren's song, daring you to dive into its depths. A chasm that darkened with every second you stared into its bottomless crux. Lightning leaped through the clouds, setting the sea aflame, white streaking through the dark sheets of the whirlpool as its force grabbed hold of *Valka*.

"Man the capstan!" my father ordered as the crew raced for the ropes. We hauled in the sails, leaving our masts—our beautiful, perfect masts—bare in the storm. The rain whipped at the wood, and the salty spray made them the perfect target for lightning. A bolt zapped across the sky, veins of light streaking down the mainmast. When the attack had subsided, the grain glowered like coals, red and orange and gold fading as the rain cooled the mast, setting the pattern in the wood, where it would remain eternally.

A rumble of thunder echoed across the waves.

"Full speed ahead! Ready the cannons! We ride through the faster waters!"

"Captain," Ray hollered over the storm. "Are you sure?"

My father glared at him, a flame flickering behind his sea-green eyes. His voice was cold when he spoke. "We ride through the faster waves. Is that clear?"

Ray stared at the ground. "Aye, Captain."

After that, no one argued against my father's insanity or how it could lead us to a miserable death. It was Captain's orders. We obeyed.

We sat on the edge of the vortex, white, frothing waves drenching our skin. As far as the eye could see, the funnel was a smooth, shiny, jet-black wall of water, consuming even the tiniest particle of foam that sprayed over its lip. The darkness sped dizzily, like the crow's nest, with a swaying and sweltering motion that could make even the most sea-worthy man hurl. The stench of decay and death rose out of the darkness, worming its way through the wood, infecting every inch of the ship.

The maelstrom had a voice too, a shrieking roar of agony that drowned out the rain, wind, and waves. A voice so powerful that it rocked *Valka*, trembling her decks. It sent goosebumps shivering up my arms.

"Hold on!" my father called out, plunging us into a nosedive.

The force swept me off my feet, and I slammed into *Valka's* side. My head flew over the edge, and my knuckles turned white as I clung to the railing. At the very tip of the funnel, I caught a glimpse of the ocean far below. It was still and dark, like deep, eternal sleep. It was the eye of the storm that the legends had spoken of, and I now wondered how many men had died at the hands of its serenity.

Then my father's hands were on my shoulders, pulling me into the safety of his embrace. Ray grabbed the wheel, righting *Valka* so she faced the direction of the whirling waters. "Are you okay?" my father asked. He was shivering, swaying as the maelstrom tried to knock us over.

It took me a moment to realize I was crying. My cheeks were already wet from the rain. I couldn't tell the difference. "Yeah," I said, my voice barely a whisper over the roaring vortex. "I'm fine." Lightning struck the heart of the whirlpool, inches away from the already-singed crow's nest.

Through the shadows, something raced to meet the electric strands, consuming the energy bite by bite until it was gone. All that remained was a dark, slimy figure towering over *Valka*.

Two massive, smoldering, flickering, ancient eyes— wholly white orbs in bone-white sockets—stared across the ocean, unblinking, sightless, yet alive with rage and terror. Their glow rebounded off the beast's teeth, row after row of blood-stained daggers that had waited thousands of years to return to the surface. I scanned the monster, looking for a body, but it was neck and more neck, all the way into the vortex.

It was a wyrm, the guardian of the maelstrom.

"Cannons to starboard!" my father ordered.

The men tore their eyes from the serpent, their feet pounding on the stairs as they staggered to the cannons below deck. I was frozen. I stood in awe, watching the legendary creature, fearing that if I blinked, it would dive back into the depths and disappear into the pages of sailor's tales. The seaspray formed a fog around its glistening body, erasing its shape briefly.

"Cannons to starboard!" my father repeated, and with the creature momentarily invisible, I came to my senses. Captain's orders. I had to obey.

Powder. Cannonball. Pack it in. Aim... Aim...

My father studied the monster, all five hundred feet of its scaled, reeking body, watching its every move. We waited for the order as the maelstrom sucked us in.

Then the beast saw us. Its flaming eyes narrowed as it roared, carrying the voice of the whirlpool in its throat, so loud I thought my ears would burst. It reared its head, ready to strike.

"Fire!" he ordered. "Fire! Fire!"

The cannons rattled, and pounds of metal struck the serpent's scales. They ricocheted off the armor, trailing fire as they plummeted into the foam and vanished.

"Keep firing! Keep firing!"

We sank further into the maelstrom, the slant of water submerging *Valka*'s right side. The starboard cannons were useless now. The spinning had caught up with us, and we held on to whatever we could so we didn't fly over the edge. I checked my lifeline as I clung to the rails. The rope was knotted firmly around the foremast.

A ripple flew down the beast's body as it turned to face us. We watched, fixated on the spectacle, like a larger version of a bull's whip. The quivering shivered down the serpent's body, all the way to its tail far below *Valka*. The wyrm thrust its tail beside the ship, throwing us into the air and out of the maelstrom.

I grabbed my lifeline as we came level with the creature.

It charged at us, opening its enormous mouth, flicking its black tongue, ready to destroy us. The jaw clamped over the ship, and a hunk of *Valka*'s side disappeared into the beast's mouth, including the rails which my father and I had been clinging to mere seconds before.

My father fell first, tumbling over the ship's edge until his lifeline stiffened. The force swung him back around, slamming him face-first against the ship's side. I thought I heard his bones shatter, but that could've been the crackling lightning overhead. It had to be.

I had a shorter lifeline, and instead of free-falling and dangling like my father, I simply dropped below the hull, the rope digging painfully into my waist.

We hung over the edge, helpless before the monster.

Pulling my line taut and placing my feet on the wood, I rappelled across the hull to where he hung motionless, face pressed against the wood.

"Captain?" I asked. "Can you hear me?" He was silent. "Are you okay?" Nothing.

The beast shook *Valka* in its teeth, slamming me hard against her side. I steadied myself by grabbing a loose board. Taking a deep breath, I swung closer to my father and turned his body around to face me. I wish I hadn't. His shirt was smeared with blood, wooden shards poking out of his chest. His face was blotchy and red, the makings of a thousand bruises scattered like constellations across his skin. My fingers found their way to his neck, checking for a pulse. It was barely there.

"Wake up!" I jiggled his shoulder gently, fearing I would break him further. I looked up at the deck. I wouldn't be able to carry him and climb at the same time.

"Oy! Get us on deck!" I ordered. They couldn't hear me over the storm.

The beast tossed us like a rag doll back into the sea. My father and I were thrown high above the ship, and we crashed through the folded mainsail before landing firmly on the deck.

I ignored the ringing in my ears and the feverish pulsing at the back of my head, turning all my attention to my father. His skin was cold, pale, lifeless.

He wasn't going to make it.

The world went silent, everything a distant echo to my ears as *Valka* tilted further, and we slid across her decks. He couldn't die. He was the Captain of *Valka*. We wouldn't survive without him. Seaspray splattered against the hot, bubbling tears streaking down my face, dripping onto my father as I held his hand firmly in mine. My heart pounded like a war drum, threatening to break out of my chest as my breath hissed against chattering teeth.

He couldn't die. We—*I* wouldn't survive without him.

The wyrm loomed over us, the whirlpool rocking the ship violently. Barrels rolled past us, almost hitting my shoulder.

"Father!" I screamed at him.

His eyes flickered open, sea-green bloodshot with red. His fingers squeezed mine gently. I sniffled back my tears. His lips moved, and I lowered my head to hear him.

"Get Ray," he whispered.

It was Captain's orders. I obeyed, shouting Ray's name until he heard.

The first mate knelt, brushing his dreadlocks away from his ears to hear my father's last orders. I didn't hear what he said, but whatever it was, it made Ray cry. It was the first time I had seen him moved to tears.

Ray staggered to his feet and took off his hat. "Yes, Captain," he whispered, his voice strained.

The beast reared its head for another attack, sinking its teeth into the ship and flipping us upside down, holding us in midair. The crew clung to what was left of the ship, but my father's injuries clouded my mind, and I only remembered to hold on to something when I had fallen past the topsail. I gripped the yard connected to the mainmast, the lightning scars creating finger holds. My father flew past me, and I grabbed his arm before he disappeared into the heart of the vortex.

"Hold on!" I yelled.

Every fiber in my body tensed as I took a deep breath and set my face, focused, ready. I tried to pull us up, using every ounce of strength, every muscle, but my father was too heavy. My fingers slipped from his rain-soaked arm, and I grabbed his wrist firmly before he fell further. I couldn't lose him. I wouldn't.

"Captain, wake up! We need you. Come on!"

I pulled again. My grip slipped. Back on *Valka*, Ray reached for our lifelines with one hand, clinging to the rails with the other, but we were out of reach.

"Captain, please." I stared down at him, searching for any sign of life. "Wake up! I need you! Come on, Father."

"Let me go. It's okay. You can't save both of us." I felt the life drain out of him as he spoke over the wind.

"Yes, I can! You just have to help."

"I can't. It's okay, Isla. Let me go."

I blocked out his voice, pulling again. A scream escaped my lips as the wyrm jolted us and my fingers slid off the mast. We fell to the crow's nest. I held onto the basket with all I had left in me, my chest heaving.

He wriggled his fingers weakly, slipping further. "Isla, stop being stubborn. Let me go."

Captain's orders.

I refused to obey.

"Stop being stubborn," I yelled over the wind. "We'll make it out of this, I promise."

I watched his face, and through the pain and agony, his expression softened. A small smile spread across his lips. He held my wrist again, which I mistook as a sign that he was listening to me, that he was going to help, that he wanted to live. He drew his sword...

"Yeah, you'll make it out of this," he wheezed. "I promise."

"Father, what are you doing?"

He raised his sword to his lifeline.

"No... No! Father, don't do this. Please!"

The blade met the rope.

"No!"

The fibers snapped one by one.

"I love you, Isla," he whispered, severing his lifeline. He let go of my wrist, and his wet fingers slithered through my grip.

My father fell into the abyss. The maelstrom whirled around him, layers of foam drowning him, and he was gone. He had become one with the sea, and there he would lie forever.

The wyrm dropped us from his teeth, sending us back toward the water.

My body dropped, heading for the deck.

Lightning struck my rope, severing it from the ship.

Detached from *Volka,* I plummeted toward the maelstrom. My arms flailed for a moment, but there was no point now. Father was gone. There was nothing worth living for anymore. I'd die with him, and that was okay.

I closed my eyes as I sank beneath the sea. I would be reunited with my family. My story would end as all the others had.

Happily ever after...

My lifeline stiffened, and I was suddenly wrenched free of the deathly clutch of the abyss. Ray held the singed end of my rope in his hands, and he yanked me toward him, placing my hands firmly on the rails.

"Thank goodness," he whispered, hugging me, running his fingers down my hair.

"No!" I couldn't remember who I was mad at. Maybe my father. Maybe the monster. Maybe me. But I took it all out on Ray as I shoved him away, battling to speak as the force of the whirlpool pinned me to the rails. "My father's gone! Your captain is gone. It's over, Ray. We've got nothing!" I shouted over the tempest.

"I beg to differ." His words were calm, an anchor in the raging current. "Isla, he named you his successor. You're the new Captain."

My arguments died in disbelief.

Me? Captain of *Valka*? My father wanted me to take the ship?

Ray gave a grim nod. "Focus, Isla. We need to find a way to launch ourselves out of this whirlpool."

I thought for a second, and a plan unfolded in my mind. I could feel the madness in my sea-green eyes, the same way my father held it in his.

"Ready the spears on starboard," I ordered. "Fasten their ropes. Wait for my command." Ray repeated it to the crew as they held the yards for dear life. As first mate, it was his duty to take control if something happened to my father. They obeyed.

The crew scaled down the masts to the weapon crates we had fastened to the decks. They wrenched out the spearguns, loading them with harpoons and knotting thick ropes over the darts. The serpent lowered its head, growling, ready to destroy us. I waited.

We drew closer to its face, a few feet away from the stench. "Hold…"

I saw its eyes, the pure, undying rage burning within them. "Hold…"

It opened its mouth, flicking its spiked tongue over the deck, howling over the waves, ready to bite.

"Fire!"

"Fire!" Ray yelled.

The crew pulled the triggers. Spears flew through the air, landing in the soft flesh just below the wyrm's jaw. It writhed in pain, wailing back at the wind. I smiled a mad, giddy smile.

"Reel us in," Ray said.

The crew fastened the spears' ropes to wheels near the mainmast, pumping the cranks, dragging *Valka* toward the monster.

Blinded by the stinging agony, the beast lost its balance, and the whirlpool sucked it in. It twirled, a broken marionette spinning on tangled strings, sending us flying around its head like a halo. As the serpent sank, we soared over the whirlpool's lip.

"Cut the lines!" I ordered. They severed the harpoon ropes on Ray's command. We hurtled across the sky like a stone from a slingshot, far away from the whirlpool, landing in a patch of the calmer seas. I looked back, searching for the serpent, but the rain surrounded us in silky curtains, blocking everything from view.

My heart raced as we sailed away in our dilapidated ship.

I grabbed the wheel, my fingers molding perfectly over the weather-worn ridges. The crew stared at me, most with eyes wide in shock, but some with grins on their faces.

"What's she doing?" a deckhand yelled. A few others

murmured in agreement.

"Men!" Ray called out, standing behind me, the wind threatening to drown his words. "Our captain has fallen, but he will not die in vain. He named his successor." The rain spat in his face, and he wiped the water off his skin. "It is my honor to present you with Isla, daughter of Captain Adrian and his wife Valka, the bravest of us all, and our new Captain!"

The deckhand who'd yelled stumbled back in shock. He turned his back to me, and some of the crew followed him. But most of them stayed.

"What now, Captain?" Ray asked, staring off into the horizon.

What would my father say to that? Something insane? Maybe. Terrifying? Probably. Impossible? Definitely.

"Let's get out of this storm first, Ray," I answered. "Fix the ship, or get a new one, and we can figure out the rest later."

"Aye, Captain," the crew shouted and got to work.

It was Captain's orders.

Ray raced to my father's quarters, *my* quarters, and returned with my father's spare tricorne and my mother's sword. I wore them proudly, tilting the hat a little over my face like my father used to.

I flung the wheel, plowing through calmer waves as the

rain subsided and the sun streaked through the darkness, down to the sea, disappearing into the depths. As the storm passed, I fingered the thin streak of blood on my arm, the cut that the wyrm's forked tongue had scarred me with.

I never knew what my father had been searching for in the maelstrom. He had made no note of it in any of his journals or maps. From all the records in his room, it seemed to be a spontaneous decision. But, after all these years, I think I had a very probable theory.

My father searched for a legacy.

I intended to do the same.

Still Waters
by Denica McCall

Over still waters rolls a gray, misty fog
Like some apparition from the past
Unwilling to part from its haunting grounds
So it lingers, like a bad taste in your mouth
The gray creeps closer, and before you're aware,
Wraps hazy tendrils around your frigid frame,
Sending ripples down your back
The foggy fingers insert their cold claims
Into your ears, your nose, your lungs
Until you choke on what remains
Mist lacks substance, you've told yourself,
But all the same, you
Struggle for breath as
This assumption proves to be a hoax
Sinking to the sandy bank, the

Denica McCall

Clouds above rumble their concurrence with your ache
Then descend upon your body,
Threatening to crush, though void of mass
You never knew that it would quell your sanity,
Never knew its pain would stand
But the still water before you makes a mockery of your
plans
Your peace has molded, your security folded
like your doubled-over self

And then you close your eyes

You draw in a sweet breath, surprising your weighted chest
The mist has fled from your mind, and
The grumble of the sky fades behind a spot of light
Though lids conceal your earthly sight,
you've blocked out these lies that taunt your mind
You can't be bested by their allegations—
You know it, suddenly, like a portent from the future:
They never had any say in your safety
For your refuge has always been found in identity, thus
Peace pushes out the gray of doubt, and
Warmth tickles up from your toes to your head
Until you're completely enveloped in love again,

A love that commands both the still waters and the waves
that rebel

You are safe, you are whole, and, dear child
You are held

This Will Not Last

by Laurel Jean

dying flower in dying light

death must come before
new life.

this death
this shedding
of all I've known must come before the rays of sun
burst bright upon my soul
to wake
a seed of what's to come.

this death
this dying will not last

this, too
this, too
this, too, shall pass.

There Isn't Much to Say
by Anne J. Hill

The lady says she's sorry for Landon's loss, and he nods a few times, mumbling his thanks. Then there's an awkward pause that feels drawn out but really must just be a couple of seconds, and the lady adds, "There isn't much to say," with a sad, knowing smile.

Landon nods. "I know." He nods again.

There's a lot of nodding at funerals.

Then she walks away and leaves Landon standing there alone in a crowd of strangers. He knows she must have also loved his sister, just like all the other unfamiliar faces dabbing their eyes and muttering goodbyes.

And he knows she didn't mean it, because there *is* a lot to say. Too much to say. Too much to fit into a superficial conversation.

In the auditorium, friends that Landon has never met and family he hasn't seen in years gather as the pastor leads them in prayer—a heavenly thanks for her life. Pictures of her time on Earth dance on the wall, and they try to share, to remember, to laugh as she would have. But there's too much to say.

It's Landon's turn to speak, but his legs won't allow him to stand. A heartbeat later, his orphaned niece pokes his arm, and his feet are moving him to the stage.

But he doesn't have much to say. To tell everything he misses, everything he's feeling, everything he's thinking would take too long and hurt too much, and there's a schedule to keep. If he were to go overtime, his sister would ask where she could submit an official complaint... if she were there.

They all nod as Landon talks because, even though they might not have been around for the stories he's telling, they can still picture her obsessive organizing and unique displays of love, because they apparently knew her, too.

Then it's over. All of it. And they make Landon and his family walk down the aisle to leave—exchanging teary smiles and nodding heads with the seated crowd. Landon reassuringly squeezes his little niece's hand. He's responsible for her now.

And there's too much to say.

A laugh pierces the heavy air as shoes plod through the sludge outside. It's been snowing, so the grass is muddy.

Another laugh. They do it because they'll cry otherwise,

and they've already done that inside.

The dearly departed's childhood friend says some words over the coffin. It's hovering above a hole, just waiting to become one with the dirt. People nod, and chuckle, and cry.

And there's too much to say, but not enough time.

Soon, too soon, she's asleep in the ground. But a thought strikes Landon's heart—something that went unsaid for most of the day. She's not truly asleep. She'll never need sleep again because that's just her body. Her soul is somewhere else entirely, laughing in controlled bursts and organizing the seasonings in the kitchen, if they have those in Heaven.

As cars drive away, Landon helps his family clean up, focusing on what needs to be done. He can cry again later, but for today his eyes are tired. So, he acts like they're just tearing down tables from a casual party—the kind his sister would have loved to plan.

And he nods and smiles because someday, he'll have plenty of time to say everything that needs to be said.

Trickster Rising
by Savannah Jezowski

"Lay of the Wing-guard"

Past the mist-moors of hel-road,
And the river ever-clanging,
Over the Watchling's bridge,
The Fence of the Fallen rises.
Death breaks the oath-bound
And ensnares the souls
Who enter by hel-gate's road.
But those who hear the song
Of sword and iron
And chase the death-realm boldly
Find the battle-hall Valhalla
Watched by the wing-guard,
Those Valkyrie shield maidens
On sky-steeds who chase the stars.

Cold nipped the boy's ears as he trudged across frozen snow. The sun dipped to the west and cast golden rays across the icy landscape. Dressed in leathers and furs, the cold didn't bother Loki.

A certain squirrel's incessant chattering, however, did. He perched on Loki's shoulder, bushy tail tickling his cheek.

"We've been down this road before." Ratatosk continued the argument they'd started that morning. It had been easy sneaking away from Odin's keep; no one particularly cared what Loki was up to as long as he got his chores done and didn't play nasty tricks on people.

Being an orphan offered few advantages, but he had more freedom than most children. He would gladly trade all that freedom for one more day with his parents.

"You saw how well it worked for you last time. We almost got eaten by a dragon," Tosk continued. "A DRAGON. You know. Big scaly beastie? Lots of teeth?" He gnashed his teeth together to imitate aggressive chomping.

"I remember." Around labored puffs, Loki wished for the hundredth time that he'd snuck away without the red squirrel. Tosk's contributions, although animated and willingly offered, proved dubiously helpful. "Thanks for the reminder though."

His first attempt to reunite with his parents at the Well

of Fate had nearly proven disastrous. He hadn't realized then the only way to find his dead parents was to enter the death-realm itself. Even the Sisters of the Well couldn't help him. But this time he was older, wiser and with a better plan.

Loki paused at a sound behind them, but it must've been ice falling from a tree.

Tosk flicked his tail and darted around a leafless birch tree to keep up with Loki's determined strides. "If not for me, you'd be a pile of bones on the Shore of Corpses, you know. My heroics and quick thinking—"

"—saved me from certain death. So you've said. Many times."

There it was again, a definite crunch of movement over frozen snow. Loki spun as a blonde girl around twelve years darted behind a gnarly oak tree.

"Odin's Beard, Signe! I told you to stay home!"

The girl popped into view, her cheeks rosy from exertion.

"You shouldn't talk about my grandfather that way." Signe waddled toward him, looking three times her usual size in her furs. She was actually quite petite, considering her heritage. With Thor for a father, her lineage boasted a great deal of muscles and beards. And her mother Sif had been a warrior princess of great renown before her death.

"You need to go back, Signe," Loki ordered, hands on

his hips. "You shouldn't be here."

The girl stopped a few paces away from him and tried to cross her arms around her bulky clothing. "You can't tell me what to do." Her sky-blue eyes blazed with her father's famous temper. "Besides, you aren't the only one who's lost someone."

A flash of black against the sky revealed a raven settling into the branches above their heads.

"Um, Loki? Signe?" Tosk said, sounding nervous. "I think—I think we've arrived."

A thick mist crawled through the forest. It was the wrong time of year for fog. These were the magical Mists that wound throughout the land, giving visions and hiding landmarks of great importance...like Helheim.

In the distance, he thought he heard the clang of metal. Loki squinted as the mists coiled toward them in an inviting yet sinister way. The silent trio stood as the echo of distant voices and sword upon sword rolled across the frigid air.

Chills crawled up his spine that had nothing to do with the cold.

"I think that's the river," Tosk whispered. He began to tug at his ear tufts, the way he always did when he was nervous. "I believe 'the river ever-clanging' is how the stories tell it. Perhaps we should reconsider this rescue mission," he squeaked. "I, uh, not that I'm afraid. Naturally—a hero of my caliber never quails before impossible odds—but death, you see, is quite a formidable obstacle, and I'd rather not greet it with open arms."

"Greet her, you mean." Loki breathed the words as if they were a curse.

"Ahem, yes." The squirrel puffed out his chest as if dredging the shallow wells of his courage. "Well, Hel isn't the queen of the dead for no reason."

Loki frowned. "It's the gate you need to worry about."

He edged forward and took one step into the Mists. The fog coiled away from him but left an unpleasantly cold wetness on his cheeks. He took another step, the Mists easing back to invite him in. The others scrambled after him, their feet and paws noisy against the snow. Soon the ground grew quiet beneath his boots as the temperature spiked and the snow melted to damp earth. Sweat gathered under his heavy furs. The clanging of the river had grown to a deafening roar when the Mists peeled back to reveal the shimmer of plunging waves and a rickety wooden bridge swaying above it.

He shed his gloves, shrugged out of his overcoat, and then peeled his woolen sweater over his head and cast that aside as well. Grunting behind him suggested Signe followed his example and stashed their clothing behind a tree. Tosk bounded to the edge of the bridge and stood with his nose in the air, tail swishing as he set a tentative paw on the wooden bridge. It creaked beneath his paws. Signe pressed against Loki's back, trying to peer over his shoulder. He hunched away from her and shot a frown at her.

"Don't hover, Sig!"

She mouthed sorry and took one tiny step backward. Loki stepped onto the bridge, right over the top of the squirrel.

The river churned beneath him, white frothing against darker, angry waters beneath the surface. Across the chasm, rocks and boulders piled high in a natural barricade, casting dark shadows against the river below.

Loki was halfway across before he noticed the hulking boulder blocking the other end of the bridge. How were they supposed to get around it? He gripped the rope railings and ignored the sickening sway.

Too late, he realized the rock wasn't a rock at all. The boulder picked itself up, stone scraping against stone, and stood before him, a craggy creature with legs, arms and chiseled face.

"You won't get by me," the rock-creature said in a grating but feminine tone. "Might as well turn around and go home."

"We need to get by," Loki announced over the clanging of the river, not believing her. Why have a bridge if people couldn't get over it?

"I will have to disappoint you then," the creature said with a noisy yawn. "I'm not supposed to let just anyone pass, you know."

Loki felt fingers tug at his elbow.

"Maybe we need to buy our way across," Signe whispered. Without waiting for a response, she stepped forward and raised her voice. "Hello, Lovely Giantess. I have this bracelet my grandfather gave me. I will trade if you let us come over." She held up a thin wrist and twisted the bracelet round and round. It was a simple thing made from a leather band and beads of varying shape and color, some carved from wood and others from bits of bone.

"It's very nice, but I have no need for jewelry." The giantess sounded tired.

"Perhaps you're hungry then?" Signe asked.

The giantess turned her craggy face toward the young girl. "Ah, now that's an idea. I haven't had a morsel in ages. Not many people come this way, you know."

Loki thought of his meager stash of food and frowned. If they wanted to have enough for the journey home, they couldn't share with the ravenous giant. Good thing he had a few tricks up his sleeve.

"Perfect!" He smiled. "We stashed some food on the other side of the bridge. If you let us pass, I'll tell you where it is."

The giantess hummed to herself as she considered. He waited anxiously until she nodded and took a lumbering step backward. "I don't know why you want to come this way, but I am very hungry."

Once they had safely scrambled past the giantess, Loki pointed across the bridge. "We hid our stash behind that rock over there."

"Thank you kindly." The giantess set a massive foot on the bridge and began the arduous journey across.

"We didn't leave our stuff behind the rock," Signe hissed as he spun, grabbed her hand, and tugged her away from the bridge.

"Which is why we need to go now." When she resisted his pull, Loki scowled. She was too tender-hearted for her own good. "Look, do you want to go home or come with us?"

Signe flinched as her expression grew resigned. "You shouldn't have lied to her," she mumbled, but this time she didn't resist when he tugged her away. "Someday you're going to regret playing tricks on people. A little shame would do wonders for you, you know."

He shrugged off her disapproval, not allowing himself to fall into regrets. He'd been lied to before, and after the incident with Nidhogg, the dragon who spun a vile deception that nearly cost Loki his life, Loki had sworn he'd never be tricked again. He would be the one doing the tricking from then on.

Surprisingly, he'd found he was rather good at it.

"She's right, you know." Tosk sniffed. "That wasn't very nice."

They hurried away from the clanging river. Skeletal trees rose on either side of the path, naked branches shivering in a stiff breeze. The ground underneath turned muddy and sucked at their boots and paws as they walked. Loki's adrenaline rose as the path wound deeper into the forest.

Abruptly, the trees fell away from the narrow road. In the distance, a stone wall rose before them, easily as tall as three men. The path angled toward an open gate where a single torch sat in a sconce on the stone, flickering an invitation.

Loki eyed the gate. Where was the gatekeeper? Remembering his encounter with Nidhogg the dragon, he was sure there had to be one and didn't relish another encounter with some dangerous creature. But after several long minutes, when no one appeared, the tension in his shoulders eased.

He rubbed his jaw and studied the high wall that ran in

both directions and disappeared into the fog. There appeared to be only one way in, and although it looked unguarded, the path couldn't be that easy. Something niggled his subconscious and filled him with the growing confidence that they did not want to walk through the gate.

Something horrible surely waited on the other side.

"Come on." He hurried, not toward the gate, but straight for the wall.

"Where are you going?" Tosk scampered to keep up.

"Over the wall."

Tosk's tail flicked back and forth in irritation. "What on earth for? There is a perfectly good entrance right over there—"

"It's a trap." Loki halted beside the massive barrier. He stripped off his boots and knotted the leather laces together. "You don't think Hel would leave the entrance to the death-realm unguarded, do you?" He slung his boots around his neck and turned his attention to the obstacle before him. It had been constructed from huge stones, the mortar crumbling and falling apart where sickly vines crawled upward and burrowed themselves between the stones. He should be able to scale the wall without too much difficulty.

"I'll toss the rope down to you." He shoved his fingers into the crevices and began to haul himself toward the top.

"It's never a good idea trying to cheat the system," Tosk

said. "It always turns out badly. We're likely to get tossed out of Helheim on our rears."

"I sincerely doubt that's the worst thing that could happen," Signe whispered. They fell silent as Loki labored his way to the top of a wall. By the time he straddled the top, his fingers and toes were scraped and bleeding, but he grinned as he tugged the coil of rope from the satchel on his back and tossed it down to the others. He descended the other side and tied his end of the rope to a gnarly old tree.

Signe soon appeared with Tosk clinging to her shoulder, his fur fluffed around his tiny body in a clear show of irritation. She rolled onto her stomach, hooked her elbows over the top of the wall, and proceeded to lower herself to the ground, muttering as her boots scrabbled against the wall. He couldn't help but grin at her lack of finesse as she dropped the last few feet and landed on her bottom with an outraged cry.

When she shot him a warning look, he wiped the amusement from his face and coiled up the rope to sling over his shoulder. They gazed around at the Mists stretching into shadows. A breeze curled around them and carried the scent of damp earth, tree bark, and something else, something unpleasant that made his nostrils curl. Other than the trees creaking in the wind, he couldn't hear a sound.

"So..." Tosk cleared his throat. "Where do we go again?"

"I have no idea." Loki adjusted his satchel. "The stories don't say anything about where to find the dead, do they?"

Tosk frowned and tugged on his ear tufts. "The tales are sorely vague on that point—bad storytelling, if you ask me."

"Maybe we need to start walking and they'll find us," Signe suggested. "They might be drawn to our presence?"

Loki shot her an annoyed look. "It's never that easy, Sig."

She flushed but held his gaze with a defiant tilt of her chin. "You don't know that."

It was never, ever that easy. One thing he'd learned as an orphan? Good things never just happened to a person. A boy had to fight for every scrap.

But since he didn't have anything else to suggest, he took Signe's suggestion and plunged wordlessly into the Mists. He had never considered how he'd locate his parents once he was here. He half-expected to somehow feel where they were. They consumed his heart with their absence. Surely, he would feel their presence?

He paused and listened as the forest creaked and the wind moaned around them, to see if he felt an inclination to go one way or another. But he felt nothing, only a terrible hollowness deep inside. His parents had left a void nothing could fill.

Signe pressed close behind him, her breathing heavy and fast.

"This place makes me feel..." Loki's whisper trailed off.

Tosk hopped onto the boy's boot and pressed close to his leg, whiskers twitching. "Bad," the squirrel supplied for him. "There are a great many other words I could use. You know, about dreadful premonitions and dire forebodings and whatnot."

"I think bad about covers it," Signe muttered.

Loki shook off the unease and took another step forward, dislodging the squirrel from his boot. Tosk scuttled ahead but glanced back at Loki. "I'd hate to get lost in this place." He twitched his tail about. "This fog is so thick I can't see my own nose."

Loki paused and glanced behind them. Already, the wall had disappeared behind a bank of fog. "Wait here a minute." He retraced his steps, uncoiling the rope from his shoulder, then knotted it to a tree right beside the wall. Once that had been accomplished, he slowly unspooled the rest of the rope as he plunged toward Signe and Tosk, who waited nervously just outside the heavy fog bank. "Here, grab hold of the rope, Sig. We'll only go as far as the rope allows and then come back and try a different route. This will keep us from getting lost."

"That's a very good idea." Signe smiled at him as if she appreciated his strengths. Most folks just saw a stick-thin boy hauling firewood to and from the forges. They didn't know him.

Not like Signe.

They'd nearly reached the end of the rope when Loki hesitated. Footsteps sucked against the damp ground while a low hum rose through the trees. It was a chilling sound, haunting like a funeral dirge, and filled his bones with an odd ache.

The humming escalated as a form emerged from the Mists ahead of them. A woman approached, swaying side to side as she sang. She stopped a few paces away and stared at them, her expression intense and calculating. The tall, plain woman was unremarkable, dressed in an old dress and cloak. She seemed young enough, but the lines around her eyes and the expression within them hinted at ancient, secret pains.

Loki knew all about that.

The woman didn't look dead either. He hadn't been sure what to expect in the death realm. Would people look the same as they had in life? Or would the marks of death be upon them? He shuddered at the thought, but if this woman was any indication of what they would find deeper in Helheim, they wouldn't have to worry about maggots and death beetles.

"I'm looking for my parents," he told her, not quite sure why he did. "Do you know where I can find them?"

"And my mother," Signe piped in, her voice trembling.

The woman swept eyes as black as midnight over Signe before returning to Loki. "You don't belong here," she said, her voice husky for a woman. "Only the dead belong here."

Another chill snaked up Loki's spine and buzzed behind his ears. The woman seemed very much alive, her movements sure and fluid, not a maggot in sight. She pointed a thin finger at him, bones prominent beneath her pale skin. "Who are you, boy?"

He swallowed a bitter taste in the back of his throat. "My name is Loki," he said as politely as he could muster. For the first time he began to doubt the wisdom of his plan.

"We meant no disrespect coming here, Lady Hel." Tosk's reedy voice pierced the uncanny stillness of the Helheim Forest. "That's your name, isn't it? You're her? The queen of the dead?"

The woman's eyes flicked to the squirrel. "Yes. And you are?"

"I am the most renowned tale-spinner in the Niflheim," Tosk said, his ears flat against the back of his head. He flicked his bushy tail and made an obvious effort to look grand and heroic and un-squirrely. "My name is

Tosk—Ratatosk, if you prefer formalities, Lady Hel, um, or is it Queen Hel? Oh dear…" He trailed off as Hel continued to pierce him with an unblinking stare.

"I've heard of you," she spoke at last, her words tinged with disapproval. "Somehow I am not surprised to see you here. You have a habit of sticking your little nose where it doesn't belong."

"Actually, I'm more in the hero business these days." Tosk revealed all his sharp little teeth in a winsome smile. What was he thinking, trying to impress the queen of death?

For the first time, Hel's expressionless features contorted into a ghost of a smile. She arched one eyebrow and dipped her head to him. "A daring pursuit for one so small."

When Signe moved from one foot to the other, Loki shot her a warning look, but it was too late. Hel's attention shifted to the young girl. "And who might you be? Are you in the hero business too?" Her words stung with mockery.

Signe lost all color in her features as Hel's gaze clasped on her. "No, ma'am, not exactly. I'm here for purely selfish reasons." The girl's voice squeaked. "I want to see my mother. I've never met her, you see. She died when I was too small to remember."

"So you thought it would be a good idea to drop by for a visit?"

"A good idea?" Signe's freckled cheeks paled. "No, probably not. But, I warn you, my father won't like it if you try to hurt me," she said in a sudden burst of bravery.

Loki had to admire her gumption.

Hel's mouth curved into a dubious smile. "And who is your father?"

"Thor Odin-son."

Hel's smile vanished, replaced instead with something dangerous and spiteful. That buzzing behind Loki's ears returned with a vengeance. He shook his head in warning to Signe, but it was too late for her to retract her words.

"You're Odin's granddaughter?" Hel asked with an incredulous laugh. "Somehow I expected someone with more meat on her bones."

Signe's pale face flamed with color. She opened her mouth with a hasty reply, but Loki surged forward to come between them. "This is all beside the point. We're here to see our parents. Are you going to let us pass or not?"

Hel glared at him, her eyes narrow, dark slits. Loki felt ill, as if the mere touch of this powerful being's gaze could snatch the very breath from his lungs. "Far be it from me to stand between you and your parents. However, if you're thinking of helping them escape, you're going to be sorely disappointed."

The shiver chilled him right to the bone. "What do you

mean?"

"The dead can't leave Helheim."

Tosk moaned loudly and yanked at his ear tufts. "I knew it. Here we go again."

Loki wasn't going to come this far only to go home empty-handed. "Why have songs been written about how to get into Helheim if rescue attempts are impossible?"

"Didn't you notice? All the songs are about how to get in...not how to get out."

"Oh, nuts and bother!" Tosk squeaked. "What is it with dragons and death monsters and an inability to lay out clear ground rules for passage? Not that you're a death monster, my good lady. You're quite pretty in a grim sort of way. But this is most inconvenient for heroes when we don't understand the rules."

Hel shot him an annoyed look. "That's the general idea. You're rather new to this hero business of yours, aren't you?"

Tosk seemed to wilt a little, his ear tufts tugged around his chin making him look ridiculous. Loki should have locked him in a pantry before he left the smithy that morning.

He shook his head and ground his teeth together. "I want to see my parents!" He spat the words. He didn't know if Hel was telling the truth, but he knew he could trust his parents.

They'd never lied to him.

"Certainly." Hel flicked her eyes to him, her expression all too eager. She held out a thin hand. "Just take my hand, and I'll bring you to them."

Something inside Loki screamed at him to back away, his fragile hopes quailing. This was too easy. Why was she so eager to help him? Being so good at tricks himself, he knew a con when he saw one. But what was her game? Her angle?

"Signe." Loki spread his feet into a firmer stance. "I think maybe you should go home now."

Hel's eyes narrowed. Something in her expression seemed almost surprised, as if she hadn't expected him to resist. His premonitions of danger only grew with each passing second.

"I'm not leaving you," Signe began, but when Loki whipped a small dagger from his belt, the girl recoiled with a squeak.

"Tosk, get her out of here," he ordered, trying to speak each word with deadly, forceful calm, so that his friends would listen to him and, for once, take him seriously. He wasn't playing a game right now, no tricks.

They needed to get out of Helheim, and they needed to get out now.

"I'll be right behind you, Sig," he promised.

Signe spun on her heels and dashed back into the Mists, following the rope back toward the wall. Her footsteps crunched across brittle leaves as she and Tosk hurried away.

"Very brave." Hel smirked as she lowered her hand to her side. She seemed unthreatened by him or his dagger. "But don't you know? Once you pass through the Gate, there is no going back. You and your little friends belong to me." Hel offered a cold smile. "So, you see, your grand attempt to save little Thor-daughter will be for nothing."

"That's just the thing." Loki tightened his grip on the dagger, his mouth curving into a sly smile. "We didn't come by way of the Gate."

For the first time, doubt clouded Hel's eyes and her lips tugged into a frown.

"Where are my parents?" Loki demanded. He didn't have many remaining hopes that Hel would help him—she seemed bent only on keeping him—but he wasn't going to leave until he'd exhausted every angle.

"You can't see them," Hel said as she returned her focus to him. Her angular nose wrinkled as her face twisted into a derisive smile. "Only the dead can see the dead. And if you didn't come by way of the Gate, then technically you aren't dead. *Yet*."

The way she said that last word, with such careful emphasis, cast a chill into Loki's bones, as if she were imagining all the ways she might make him dead.

The goddess of death moved so suddenly Loki barely had time to respond. He lashed out with his dagger as the woman surged toward him, her claw-like fingers wrapping around his wrist. An aching cold began to sweep through him, creeping up his arm, past his elbow, toward his shoulder. He tried to strike her with the dagger, but he'd never stabbed anyone before, and at the last moment, the moment that mattered most, he faltered.

Hel's other hand closed around his throat, and the cold washed over his entire body, into every vein, every bone, every nerve.

Light flashed around him. Was it stars in his vision as he passed from life into the realm of the dead?

He didn't know. He only knew when Hel released him, and he sat down hard on his rump.

"What are you doing here?" Hel's voice pierced the fog of his confusion. She sounded angry, annoyed. "This one is mine, Kára."

"No, he's not," another voice replied, as different from Hel's husky tones as night was from day. Loki focused on a broad-shouldered woman in white furs and leathers dyed in deep, golden tones. Wavy blond hair decorated with beads and white feathers swirled in an invisible breeze, brushing against the round shield strapped across the newcomer's back. Behind her, something stamped against the ground. Loki's mouth fell open when he saw the horse. Only it wasn't a horse, but some creature with feathered wings folded against its snow-white flanks.

He scrambled to his feet and back a few steps. He'd only heard about such creatures in legend. The wing-steeds, the mounts of the...this could only mean one thing. The woman bearing the crest of the swan was a Valkyrie.

"He's mine, you feathery pest! He's a foolish boy who walked willingly to his own death!" Hel frowned and crossed her arms over her chest. Her voice had taken on a wheedling tone that seemed oddly inappropriate for a queen of death realms. "Kára. He's mine."

The Valkyrie, Kára, shook her head. "He sacrificed himself to save his friends. He died on the field of battle."

Hel groaned and threw her hands out in a helpless gesture. "Now you're grasping, Wing-guard. I'd hardly call this—" She waved a hand toward Loki. "—a field of battle. Just scrubby trees and a stupid little boy."

Loki drew himself up. "I'm not stupid. I came over the wall. You can't keep me here because I didn't walk through your stupid gate. I tricked you."

Hel's eyes narrowed, but instead of recoiling in indignation, she smiled. "Perhaps you aren't as clever as you think." She held up her hand, the very one that had grabbed him moments before. She turned it slowly side to side, as if admiring the ghostly hue and slender shape. "One touch is all it takes." Loki's heart began to pound as he recalled all too clearly the bitterness of her touch, the coldness that raced through his body.

She looked at him then, smug and cold and awful.

She wasn't lying. Somehow, Loki could feel it in his bones that something wasn't quite right.

"If he didn't come by way of the Gate," Kára began, her sky-blue eyes sweeping over Loki as she contemplated, "then you had no right to touch him. You broke the rules, Hel."

"Oh, you and your dratted rules!" Hel argued. "It doesn't matter how he got here."

Kára shook her head once slowly. "Oh, but it does." She held out a scarred hand toward Loki. He darted forward all-too-eagerly and grasped it, knowing his fate rested in the hands of this woman. Her touch drove the chill from his bones and flooded him with delicious heat.

Calling this woman a feathered pest seemed a gross injustice. The Valkyrie was a vision of beauty and strength, with kindness radiating from her eyes and a gentle smile. How strange that a person could seem so strong and gentle at once.

Loki had always assumed a person could only be one

thing. Strong or gentle. Clever or kind.

For some reason he thought of the giantess he'd so cruelly tricked. Guilt surged inside him as loudly as the clanging of the river. Kára smiled, as if she could see through him, right down to his secret thoughts, his secret guilts.

He'd never been so ashamed.

"I don't want to give him up!" But Hel's voice had lost its conviction, as if she knew she'd already lost. "This one's halfway clever. I haven't had a clever one in ages. Please, let me keep him."

Loki shot her a panicky look and shrank against Kára's side. The woman squeezed his palm as if to reassure him. Without answering, she turned and walked back to her winged horse, with Loki scrambling to keep up. Kara released his hand and threaded her fingers together, making a step for him to swing up onto the horse. He crawled across the creature's back and awkwardly settled in.

"This isn't fair!" Hel called. She looked small and dark and insignificant, surrounded by Mists and shadows. How was it that she had looked so menacing only moments before?

Kára swung up behind Loki and grabbed two fistfuls of mane. "When have you ever concerned yourself with fairness, my dear?"

Hel's expression froze as her eyes dropped to the

ground. She looked like a whipped pup caught in some mischief. For a moment, Loki actually felt sorry for her.

Then the horse pranced in a circle and launched off powerful hooves. Loki whooped as air rushed through his dark hair, tossing it wildly around his face. Kára said nothing as she guided the horse through the midnight sky, above the Mists, over the wall, and then down into a small clearing near the bridge.

Signe and Tosk waited for him, their mouths open in shock as he slid off the side of the horse and stepped away from the Valkyrie. Kára dipped her head to him, her smile soft but tinged with sadness.

"You're free to go," the Valkyrie said, but she lifted a finger in warning. "But don't think that you've escaped unscathed, dear boy. Death has seen you now. There's no escaping that. She'll come for you, perhaps sooner than you might wish. I suggest you make no more forays into death realms."

Loki's eyes fell to his feet. If he gave up on his quest to be reunited with his parents, he'd never see them again. He'd be alone for the rest of his life.

He blinked away tears and tried to hide them behind his hand, embarrassed.

Boots hit the ground moments before a firm hand squeezed his shoulder. "You can't get them back," the woman said quietly. "You need to let them go."

Signe began to cry, making Loki's tears flow more freely. He rubbed them away with his arm. "I don't want to be alone," he begged. "Please, isn't there a way?"

Kára shook her head, her feathered and beaded hair wafting about her shoulders. "You're not alone." She swept her other hand toward Signe and Tosk. Signe sniffed and darted forward to throw her arms around his waist. She pulled back, her face reddened as if she'd spent too much time in the sun.

"Sorry," she said. "I know you don't like hovering."

Kára smiled and rested her other hand on Signe's shoulder. "If you wish to know your mother," she said as she leaned forward to peer into the girl's face, "just look in the mirror, my dear girl. You have her eyes and her spirit. Treasure that. It will sustain you."

Signe choked back a sob and scrubbed a fist against one eye and then the other. She mumbled a thank you as she battled to control herself.

Tosk cleared his throat and scampered to perch on the Valkyrie's boot. Loki marveled at his gall. "What about me? Do you have any words of wisdom for me?"

Kára smiled and lowered a hand to pat him behind the ears. "Perhaps you should take better care of your friends. Heroes don't always fight battles, you know. Sometimes they just keep their loved ones out of death realms."

Tosk grabbed one of his ear tufts and fiddled with it as he scuttled backward. "I see." He stirred the dirt with one of his back paws. "That rather does sound like wise advice." He coughed and eyed Loki sheepishly.

Kára straightened. "Ah, it seems you have another matter that needs your attention," she said. Loki followed the direction of her gaze and saw a massive stone giant looming at the entrance to the bridge, looking dejected and forlorn. "I hope you'll choose to be kinder in the future." Her stern eyes settled on Loki.

He swallowed hard and nodded. Making amends wasn't something he was good at, but he had a feeling he'd be doing it a great deal in the future.

Kára climbed onto her mount and waved one more time before her wing-steed broke into a trot and took to the skies. The trio watched in awed silence until the beating of mighty wings vanished into the night.

"Well," Tosk began, "I hope you've learned a valuable lesson today."

Loki slanted him an annoyed look. Yes, he'd learned his lesson, but he rather didn't want to be beaten about the ears with it.

"You should've packed more supplies." Tosk eyed the giant between them and safety. "I fear that old girl is going to be in a ravenously ill-humor."

Loki rolled his eyes, but when Signe grabbed his hand and squeezed, he met her gaze and scratched his jaw with a rueful smile. "I know," he said, sounding as sheepish as he felt. "You don't have to say it. I'm ashamed."

She beamed at him.

As he turned to face the giant, Loki prepared the humblest sort of apology he could imagine. Signe gave his hand another squeeze before releasing him to do what he needed to do.

Clever and kind.

Overhead, Odin's raven watched as they turned to follow the winding path back to the bridge and its stone guardian. The raven stirred from the branches of a skeletal tree and lost itself in the overcast sky, it's watchful task complete.

Part Two:

A Slash of Humor

The Headless Henwoman
and the Kissing Curse
by Kristiana Sfirlea

I drive a carriage pulled by headless chickens for a living. Well, *living* is an interesting word. So is *dead*. Technically, I'm neither. I'm a Collector of Souls, an agent of the heavenly realms and netherworlds alike. Or that's my official title, anyway. Me? I like to go by Heehee the Headless Henwoman.

And today, this Heehee has a job to do on a wet, lonely road in Ireland.

My carriage—a giant handbasket on wheels—materializes in the mud of O'Spritely Lane. (Named, I should note, for its plethora of otherworldly activity and not for the deliciously fizzy beverage.) I've delivered many a lost soul from this road and its surrounding forest, and my chickens know the path well. You might not think it from the way they run about, pulling in all different directions, but do keep in mind: *they're chickens with their heads cut off.* Driving them is a skill best undertaken by someone with their own detachment problems. Such as me.

One hand keeps a firm grasp on the reins, and the other props my decapitated head on my hip. I scan the scenery, searching for the object of my assignment. When nothing catches my eye, my hand grips my hair and lifts my head high in the air for a better vantage point.

Nope. Still nothing.

"Where are you, my chick?" I murmur. It's dusk out, the perfect time to meet a Lady in White. They're timid ghosts, generally speaking, usually seen weeping and wandering along the roadside. Even in death, they are beautiful, dressed in anything from dazzling wedding gowns to elegant night robes. All white—save for the bloodstains.

Pitiful creatures, Ladies in White. They don't speak much, too caught up in the sorrow of their tragic ends, which typically includes a scorned lover, a jealous lover, a long-lost lover, or a dead lover. Pick any noun or adjective and slap the word *lover* next to it, and you have your basic Lady in White backstory. (My personal favorite? Burger lover. Who wants to die choking on their favorite meal? Chew your food, for hen's sake! Your life might just depend on it.)

I wonder what my current Lady in White's history

involves. Knowing where they come from can help convince them to leave this mortal world and enter eternity with me. You can imagine the challenge of persuading someone to get into a giant handbasket pulled by a headless brood of chickens—particularly when the driver herself is headless. Some ghosts are so eager to leave their entrapment on earth that they'd hop into the death coach of the Dullahan himself. But not Ladies in White. They're too enamored with their own sadness, glorying in their weeping, in the cold beauty of their decadent white death clothes, in their refusal to speak of anything except the sorrow of their—

"Oi! Watch where you're going!" shouts an Irish girl, and my chickens swerve (more than normal, that is). I yank on the reins, pulling my basket on wheels to a halt.

The girl marches over, hands on her hips, and stops in front of the carriage, a roadblock whose stance reminds me of someone about to do the Chicken Dance. The idea brings a smile to my disembodied head. Mistake—the girl seems even angrier now.

"What are you smiling about?" she growls. "You almost ran me over! I've already *been* run over, and I'd prefer not to replicate the experience, thanks."

The girl looks around seventeen with long, dark hair spilling over her shoulders. She's wearing a cotton tee and lounge pants.

White cotton tee and lounge pants.

It can't be...can it?

It has to be. Only ghosts and other supernatural entities can see me and my chickens.

This is my Lady in White.

I give a *heehee* of a laugh. "You're not what I was expecting."

The girl crosses her arms over the tire marks on her shirt. "Well, *you're* not what *I*—" The words die in her throat. She notices my headless chickens for the first time. Her eyes travel up to the jagged, gaping wound that is my neck, then to my head held up like a lantern in my hand. The girl's see-through skin blanches a white so impossible only a ghost could manage it. "Are you the Dullahan?"

I snort. "Do I look like a headless horseman? Does my basket look like a death coach? Do my chickens look like beheaded steeds? I may look like a hazing ritual gone horribly awry"—I glance down at my gown and the feathers stuck to it by the congealing red blood from my head and neck wounds—"but no, I am not the Dullahan. I'm Heehee the Headless Henwoman."

It's the ghost girl's turn to snort. "Heehee? Your mam had a sense of humor."

"She thought I was a hoot."

"I thought chickens cock-a-doodle-*dooed*."

"I'm not a *dude*. I'm a Collector of Souls, and I'm here to help you move on into eternity. What's your name, my chick?"

The ghost girl lets her arms drop to her sides. "Sable. Are you really going to help me move on? 'Cause I am *so* bored. I don't even know why I came back. One minute I'm being run over by a car, and the next, I'm doomed to walk the same road every night for the rest of my afterlife."

A ghost that doesn't know why they came back? Unusual. But everything about this Lady in White has been unusual. Gosh, I love a rule-breaker.

I pat the handle of my handbasket carriage. "Well, climb on in, Sable! We'll get you out of here in no time." I can't believe how easy this is. No fighting, no chasing, no arguing, or persuading—just a ghost wanting to move on and a Heehee willing to help her.

It warms my not-quite-living, not-quite-dead heart.

Sable is about to ghost through the side of my carriage when she stops. Grins. "Gives a whole new meaning to going to hell in a handbasket, doesn't it?"

I laugh again. Yes, I've heard that one a million times. No, it hasn't gotten old. "The saying came from somewhere, you know." I wink.

Her ethereal form glides through the thick, woven

material of the carriage, and she positions herself next to me, ghostly fingers running across the rim of our unconventional transport. "But seriously. Why do you drive a giant basket?"

"Because I'm Heehee the Headless Henwoman, and souls are like eggs," I say. "Fragile and full of life. What better thing to gather them in and transport them safely where they need to go?"

"And where *are* we going? To hell in a handbasket?" Sable's voice is calm, playful even, but she fiddles nervously with a crucifix around her neck.

"Not to worry. Hold on to your faith, and all will be well. It's time for us to leave this world. To eternity... and beyond!" I snap my reins with a satisfying *crack!*

My chickens refuse to move.

I clear my throat. "I said—and with just the right touch of dramatic flair, I might add—to eternity...and beyond!" Another snap of the reins.

One chicken lets out a gurgling squawk from its severed throat. Another flutters its wings. The rest of them nestle down on the road like broody hens.

Sigh. And this was going so well. I turn and brace my head on top of my neck so that I'm eye-to-eye with my ghost girl. "Sable, my chick, we need to have a talk about your love life."

Sable's eyes narrow dangerously. "Talk about my *what*, now?"

"You're a Lady in White, a girl who died wearing white clothes and is stuck here because of some love affair with a man or, occasionally, cheese."

She purses her lips thoughtfully. "I do love a good cheddar."

"Were you eating it while you died?"

"No."

"Then that's probably not why you're here. Think about what you were thinking about when you were dying. Was it a boy? A burger? There's no need for embarrassment. Whatever the longing that made you a Lady in White, I've seen them all."

Sable's nostrils flare impressively. "And where do you get off asking me personal questions? I haven't even asked you why you're *headless*!"

"If I answer your question, will you answer mine?" I challenge.

"Maybe."

Better than no. "All Collectors of Souls are headless, as are their beasts of burden. There was a revolt in eternity past, and when it ended, the winners decided that we Collectors needed a change in perspective." I lift my head off my neck and spin it around by my hair. "Tada! The wounds won't heal until the time for collecting souls is over. Then the reminder of our mistakes will be taken away, and the contrite will take their place in the heavenly realms while the wicked will join the misery of the netherworlds."

Sable nodded. "So there are good Soul Collectors and bad Soul Collectors. And you're one of the good ones, I take it? Do you only collect good souls?"

"My job is to help souls move on, wicked or contrite. I go where I'm called and deliver souls to the destinations they chose by what they put their faith in."

She clutches her crucifix once more. "And...what about the Dullahan?"

A shiver runs down my back like the tickling of a feather. I can almost hear the violent snorts of his headless horses, the implacable trudge of his death coach down O'Spritely Lane. I've seen my share of appalling apparitions, but nothing compares to the sight of the Dullahan. His body encased in the blackest leather, his head swinging from a gauntleted fist. A face that might once have been handsome were it not for the scars and the blaze of his hellfire eyes—and, of course, the whole not-attached-to-his-body thing.

But his appearance alone was not the source of his infamy.

"The Dullahan," I say, "collects the souls of anyone

who is under a curse. That is his special job and one he relishes." I shiver again, and my head wobbles on my neck. I remove it, tucking it securely under my arm. "Now, I've answered your question—time to answer mine. We need to find out what's keeping you here. You're a Lady in White, so it probably has something to do with a romantic attachment. What lover is keeping you tied to this mortal world?"

Ghost blush is such a pretty color: bright white with just a tinge of translucent pink. "I don't have any *lovers*," Sable grits through her teeth. "I don't—I'm not—romance doesn't interest me, okay? I've never even had a boyfriend. I just like...dogs. And drawing cartoons. And my friends. And my family. That's enough for me. And don't you *dare* tell me I'm missing out on love because I love all of them *so much*. And I miss them like you wouldn't believe, but they're not what's keeping me here. I didn't want to die, but I didn't fear it either because my greatest love is waiting for me in heaven." She kisses the cross of her necklace and lets it fall back on her chest. "I just didn't realize it would take so long to get there."

"Oh, Sable." I reach out and touch her ghostly shoulder. It's as cold as the grave. "There are all different kinds of love in this world, but when you know the Source of love itself, you are never lacking." A thought crosses my mind, and my arm freezes as if her ghost touch has turned it to ice. "But you've truly never had a boyfriend?"

That ghost blush again, but there is a determined set to her jaw. "Nope!" She even pops the *p*.

My senses flip to high alert, and I raise my head up by my hand to survey our surroundings. Was the forest on either side of the road always so still? And that sound on the breeze. Could it be...? "I have a very important question for you, and you *must* answer it no matter how uncomfortable it makes you."

"O-kaaay." She looks at me askance.

"Have you ever been kissed?"

Amazingly, she smiles. Relief whooshes through me, and I lower my head. No doubt she is remembering the awkwardness, the blissfulness of a first romantic kiss. And oh, look, she's even going to tell me the story!

"I was twelve," Sable begins, "and his name was Conor Doyle. He was cute, in a scruffy sort of way, and we were behind the swing set at school. We were talking about the differences between cat and dog owners—he had cats, I had dogs—and right after my passionate dissertation on the disgustingness of hairballs, he leaned in to kiss me."

"And?" I prod.

"And..." She pauses for a beat, a mischievous quirk to her lips. "I stomped on his foot and kneed him where it hurts. Word spread quickly after that, and I never had to worry about a boy trying to kiss me ever again!"

I want to smile with her, to laugh with her, to whisk her safely away into eternity where her greatest love is waiting. But I can do none of these things, and finally, I know why.

"Oh, my dear Sable." Head tucked under my arm, I grab her ghost-cold hands in mine. "I'm afraid you have something else to worry about." I can hear it clearly now, the unflinching *clip-clop* of horses on the road. I feel his presence in the dread coiling in my stomach like a writhing snake. He's coming. He's coming for *her*. "My chick, you are cursed."

Sable wrenches her hands free. "I'm *what?*"

"You died without ever being kissed."

There is fire in her eyes to match the Dullahan's. "And how is that a curse? Who comes *up* with these things? First, we tell girls they have to kiss frogs to get princes, which, peel back a couple layers of metaphor, is basically telling them they're in charge of transforming boys into moral, civilized human beings—as if boys are intrinsically frogs and girls are intrinsically responsible for their humanity. And now you're telling me that because I've never kissed—boy *or* frog—I'm cursed? I've read the Good Book. There's nothing in there about a kissing curse!"

"It's not a curse from above. It's a curse from below. We have to move, now! Take my head." I pass her my decapitated noggin and take hold of my chickens' reins. They can't move us into eternity, but they can still *move*. "Come on, my chicks. Let's show that horseman how fast headless chickens can *really* run." I crack the reins, and this time, the birds hop to their feet and charge! Granted, in several different directions, but it gets my basket on wheels moving. Before long, we are swerving down O'Spritely lane at breakneck speed.

Amazing how quickly someone can catch up to you when they don't have a neck to break.

My head is held just beneath Sable's chin, and I feel it brush my hair as she looks behind us and swears. "It's the Dullahan! He's coming!"

"Show me."

She boosts my head up and turns me around. Sure enough, thundering in our wake is the Headless Horseman himself, spurring his beheaded steeds on at a harrowing pace. His death coach trundles behind him, a monstrous black box full of dead things. The Dullahan lifts his disembodied head high in the air, like a victory flag.

He hasn't won anything. Not Sable's soul—not if this Heehee has anything to say about it.

"He's catching up." My ghost girl's voice wavers.

"What happens if I go with him? Will he still take me to heaven?"

"The Dullahan isn't allowed in the heavenly realms, not even to deliver souls," I tell her. "That's why he's in charge of the cursed. They almost always make their home in the netherworlds."

"But I won't! I'm supposed to go to heaven!" She holds my head at eye level, and iridescent tears glisten on her ghostly cheeks. She looks ready to tear the crucifix from her neck. "Why is this happening? Why would He even let me be cursed?"

"I don't know," I admit. "But He hasn't abandoned you."

"How do you know?"

I smile at her, ignoring the blood from my severed neck trickling down her arms. "Because He sent me, didn't he? Now, all we have to do is figure out how to break your curse, and the Dullahan will leave us alone."

Sable sniffs and wipes her nose on her arm. My blood smears her ghostly cheek. "And how do I break the curse? By kissing someone?" By the look on her face, you'd think someone had asked her to lick a toilet seat.

"That's an option," I say gently, "but there's a catch. A kiss from a Lady in White is a deadly thing. Your first kiss could be someone's last. But if that someone was neither living nor dead..." An idea pops into my mind. Oh, Sable's gonna love me for this.

I explain my idea to her. She shares her opinion with me. It's a cordial conversation minus the profanity. But it's a choice between heaven or hell, and Sable's made her decision.

I let out a string of clucks, and my headless body pulls on my chickens' reins. They slow to a stop. The thundering hooves of the Dullahan's headless horses follow suit, and his death coach parks behind my basket. Waiting.

Sable hands my head back to my body, takes a deep breath—pointless, of course, but an old habit of living—and ghosts through the side of our carriage.

"You can do this, my chick," I whisper to her.

She nods and puckers her lips (whether in consternation or preparation is unclear) and strides confidently to the Dullahan's death coach. "May I see your head, please?" She holds her hands out expectantly. "I promise not to use it as a football."

The Dullahan blinks. He probably isn't used to this sort of reaction from his assignments. People begging for their lives? Sure. People screaming and running at the sight of him? Just another day on the job. But someone asking to see his head?

Amazingly, for the sheer novelty of it, perhaps, he

156

obliges.

Sable lifts his head, scarred and handsome, with both hands so that his hellfire eyes are level with hers. She stares into them unflinchingly. "A little headless birdie told me you think I'm cursed because I've never kissed anyone. Well, guess what, Mr. Headless Horseman?" She leans in close, screwing up her face as if he has slugs for lips. I fight down a *heehee*. This is no laughing matter, no matter how laughable her expression.

A henpeck. That's all she needs to break this curse. A *henpeck*.

Can she do it?

At the last second, *the very last second*, Sable pulls back. It's hard to tell with the scars and the blazing eyes like a jack-o-lantern, but the Dullahan looks...disappointed.

"Here's what I'm going to tell you. Are you listening? I." She boops his nose once. "Am not." She boops it again. "Cursed." A third, unforgiving boop. "You think your curses apply to me, but they don't. I'm not part of your world—I'm part of a better one. That's where I'm going now, and you can't stop me. The only reason I got stuck here in the first place is because somehow, deep down, maybe I believed in your curse, that somehow my life was unfinished because I'd never been kissed. Belief is a powerful thing. But you know what? I don't believe it anymore. My life may have been short, but it was real, and it was full of love. You wanna know why? Because I know the Source of love itself, and I'm going to Him now. Nothing you do or say can change that. So you can take your headless horsies and your death coach and go back to hell."

I cheer from my basket and clap my hands, promptly dropping my head on the woven floor. Oops. I pick it back up in time to see Sable toss the Dullahan's head back at his body. He catches it and stumbles back, cowed by her confidence.

"A kiss from me won't save you, Mr. Headless Horseman. Only you can make the choice to change from a frog to a prince. And next time you pick up a cursed soul, remember: curses, like chickens, come home to roost." Sable salutes him and rejoins me in my giant basket on wheels.

"How do you feel, my chick?" I ask her warmly, head propped on my hip.

She grins, brushing stray feathers from her cotton tee and lounge pants. "I'm good. I'm grand. I'm ready to go to *heaven* in a handbasket."

I crack the reins, and my headless chickens pull us every which way into eternity.

Misconception

by Savannah Jezowski

They call her a witch, that raven-haired girl
who lives in the stone cottage
deep in Aspen Wood,
the haunted forest, buried in shadow
and faerie blight.
Only a witch would live alone,
they say,
in the company of dragons
and faeries and changeling folk, those
tricksters and demons.
She's a witch, they say, with raven hair
and dragon eyes.

Beware the dragon witch
who lives in Aspen Wood—
she has dragon eyes,
they say.

Savannah Jezowski

Eyes the color of the forest
must be dragon eyes, for sure.
One glance from them will entrance
the most fearless woodsman
and lure him, bespelled, deep
into the heart
of Aspen Wood
across a floor of human bones
and moldy skulls,
into the humid throne room
where sleeps the dragon lord
on his bed of pilfered treasure.

Beware the dragon witch
who lives in Aspen Wood—
she has such eyes,
they say.

The village children who dare to visit
lurk in the shadows and peer
from behind trees.
The bravest throw rocks at her windows,
tromp through the flower beds
and pull feathers from the tails
of chickens

while she wanders the forest,
gleaning herbs from her
secret gardens.
They go home with chilling tales
of a boiling cauldron
and bone wind chimes.

Beware the dragon witch
deep within Aspen Wood—
the one picking rowan berries
for jams.

Literary Lies

by Kat Heckenbach

She stared o'er the corpse, looking startled.
Its flesh curled from bone, burned to charcoal.
She said, book in hand,
"I don't understand...
Shouldn't the sun make him sparkle?"

It's Alive!

by Anne J. Hill

I paced my shadowy apartment, anticipation welling up inside of me. Today was the day I'd waited an entire three business days for. Today, my package would be delivered.

I'd arranged everything for this moment. My preschooler was having quiet time in his room; I'd cleared a space on the "Shelley" labeled section of my bookshelf; my hands were clean in preparation for holding the most precious merchandise.

A knock on the front door reverberated down my spine, and I rushed to open it, giggling like a child on Christmas morning. Nothing would be the same after today. My collection would be complete.

I threw open the door and beamed down at the box on my porch—a basic package in most regards, other than the tape that seemed to patch together pieces of various cardboard to make one box, and the flowing script that adorned the lid:

Bard's Beguiling Bookstore

"Hello, precious!" I said as I swooped it up in my arms and slammed the door shut. "We're going to be the best of friends forever, you and I."

I set the box down on the kitchen counter, then pulled out a sharp knife and slashed away the tape, desperate to get to my prize. Pushing back the flaps, I squealed a little and lifted the contents free.

Frankenstein. Second edition. Leatherbound, with only a single crack along the spine.

I shivered with excitement and ran my fingers over the rigid cover. "Well, hello there, Frankie Number Twelve." I tossed the cardboard box in the trash and settled onto the couch by the crackling fireplace to examine the newest member in my *Frankenstein* collection.

The spine creaked as I opened it and took in a deep sniff. At the smell of well-loved and then long forgotten pages, I couldn't help but smile. Few things in life could beat that aroma. The feather-edged pages passed through my fingers, and I admired the thickness of each leaf. I glanced up fondly at the space on my bookshelf between edition one and edition three.

I hugged it like it was an old friend, breathed in the cozy

scent of book and fireplace, wiggled my toes in my slippers, and basked in the completeness of my collection. Everything was perf—

Something plastic rustled in the kitchen.

I froze, glancing toward the noise.

Thud dum.

"H—Hello?" I swallowed fear down my tightening throat.

Nothing.

Taking a deep breath, I stood and tiptoed to the kitchen, squeezing my new book to my chest. All was quiet—nothing amiss.

Nothing except the misshapen cardboard box sitting on the floor.

I laughed. "Oh, goodness. You must have fallen out. You're not allowed to scare me like that." I smashed it down with my slipper-clad foot and stuck it back into the trash can. "Now, you stay put."

Only it didn't.

The second I turned, I nearly screamed at the sound of cardboard hitting the floor behind me.

I moved slowly back around, eyes wide in horror. There was nothing unique about the smashed box on my floor.

Except that it'd moved there on its own.

I grabbed salad tongs from the counter and poked the thing. Nothing happened.

"All right, mister." I pointed accusatory tongs at it. "You stay in the trash can like a good little box and stop being alive and creepy. Got it?"

The box looked sad, and I took that as a yes. The salad tongs gripped onto the cardboard, and I dropped it back in the trash can. This time I did not turn my back, keeping my unblinking eyes trained on the Frankenstein impersonator. The trash can and I had a good two-minute staring war until I sighed and turned to go back to the couch, cursing my overactive imagination.

Thud dum.

I spun around and threw the tongs at the cardboard that'd appeared back on the ground.

I missed by a mile, but the box still looked offended.

"What do you want, you little cardboard Frankenstein!" I tossed my hands in the air. The box said nothing because it was, well, a box.

I eyed the thing while pacing back and forth. "One more chance, mister. If you jump out again, I'll throw you in the fireplace! Understand?"

The box looked like it did understand, so I retrieved the tongs to drop it back into the trash. I brushed success off my hands and started back to the living room.

"But you said we're best friends..." a small, muffled male voice said.

My heart jolted in my chest, my left foot freezing in mid-air. I whirled around to see the box back on the floor.

"No. No, no, no." I shook my head, trying desperately to rattle the temporary insanity from my brain. Snatching up the tongs, I carried the box to the fireplace and, without any hesitation, tossed it into the flames. "Begone, possessed box!"

As the cardboard curled into ash, the thudding in my chest slowed.

"I'm never buying from *Bard's* again!" I proclaimed and flung myself, finally, back on the couch.

"Mommy?" The voice, now crisp as day, came from the kitchen. I shoved off the couch and poked my head into the room. What I saw made me first jump, then keel over in fits of laughter.

Standing in the trash can with a banana peel for a hat and rotten avocado smeared on his face was my mischievous preschooler.

"You're supposed to be napping, mister!" I scolded with a smile.

He giggled and rubbed at the avocado on his cheek. "This was more fun."

I pulled him out of the trash and kissed his forehead.

"At least I can still buy books from *Bard's*!"

He nodded as I finally slid my new edition into its slot on the bookshelf, and I whisked away my Frankenstein impersonator to take a bath.

Immortals Anonymous
by Megan Mullis

On Friday mornings,
tired monsters shuffle in,
each opening the door and letting it fall shut,
each quietly conversing as they wait not so patiently.

On Friday mornings,
tired monsters take their seats,
in little plastic chairs,
lined up in organized rows of two,
facing the microphone,
in their little quiet chapel room.

On Friday mornings,
tired monsters drink their coffee,
sighing and grunting,
or quietly complaining,
to the tired monster next to them,

who is perhaps nibbling a cookie,
or shuffling their feet anxiously,
never too tired for last minute stage fright.

On Friday mornings,
tired monsters take their turns,
stepping up to the podium,
each player struts the stage,
waiting for their moment to say,
"Hi, my name is Clark,
and I've been a vampire for a hundred and fifty years"

On Friday mornings,
a tired audience echoes back,
and just like that,
an apprehensive monster begins to talk,
not about bad coffee or early morning meetings,
but about feeling lonely,
how tiresome it can be to be a monster,
how long forever is,
how the days drag on,
they listen in response,
and suddenly,
an anxious vampire is less alone.

Immortals Anonymous

On Friday mornings,
a ghost does not like his new roommates,
he doesn't want to kill them,
he just doesn't like that they leave the cabinets open,
a skeleton does not like being the symbol for death,
even if he is dead,
a lizard man scratches at his scales that are perpetually dry,
and a banshee cries.

On Friday mornings,
tired monsters commiserate,
they find common ground in their plastic seats,
and even so different,
they are all tired,
and they are all monsters,
and there's something freeing about community.

Don't Feed the Leprechauns
by Lara E. Madden

Red desert stretched to the horizon as the green rental car kicked up a trail of dust along New Mexico's Route 14. The couple in the car had been driving since the early hours of the morning and were now twenty minutes past Santa Fe, heading south toward some national forest that the husband had never heard of. They were one week into their anniversary vacation, and this was their third year of marriage, so in some respects, they were still newlyweds, but they had been married long enough to have lost their shyness around loud arguments. Currently, they were running low on caffeine, gas, and patience.

"Hun, we're in a desert. It's a hundred and twenty degrees outside—this is why air conditioning exists!" The man was talking loud and fast.

His wife, on the other hand, spoke with an infuriating calm, as if explaining something simple to a child. "It's not a hundred and twenty degrees. It's a hundred and *two* degrees. And that's the *outside* temperature, babe. *In the car,* it's only seventy-five."

"But it could be *sixty*-five, and you could put on a jacket, and then we'd both be happy!"

The wife pursed her lips and referred back to the "driver chooses the temperature" rule her husband had set earlier. When *he* had been driving.

The man rolled his eyes and grunted, but didn't continue to argue. He clicked the radio on and turned the dial, his frustration growing with every fuzzy and static-drowned station he tried.

Finally, his wife hit the radio's power button. "Driver chooses the audio, too."

Her husband threw up his hands, then crossed his arms over his chest and flopped back in his seat. "Wake me when we get there," he grumbled.

Blue mountains rose in the distance to their left and right, and far down the flat road were the very faint outlines of long buildings. Now and then, a traffic sign or a passing truck or a piece of tumbleweed broke the monotony, but otherwise, the road was solitary and quiet.

The husband mumbled something under his breath.

"Hmm?"

"I said I don't know how you convinced me to spend

my vacation days in this place."

"Babe, it was your idea!"

"No, it was *your* idea! I never wanted to come here. You were going on and on about how I never listen to anything you say, and we never go anywhere you want to go, so I *listened,* and we came *here*."

"I'm missing your point," she said.

"This is not somewhere you vacation! It's a wasteland—"

"Now hang on!"

"It's where you go when you can't go anywhere else; when you're running from the law or trying to hide from someone or something."

"It's beautiful."

"It's a *desert*." He rolled his eyes and glanced out the window for half a second-

"Watch out!" The man reached across to the steering wheel and jerked it to the left, swerving the car into the other lane to avoid a hitchhiker.

The wife slammed on the brakes, and the car came to a stop a dozen yards down the road. They were both panting from the sudden burst of adrenaline, and they looked like they were trying to decide whether to laugh or cry or scream at each other.

"He just came out of nowhere," the wife croaked. Her

husband nodded, his eyes still wide. He let out a breathy, relieved chuckle.

The wife adjusted her rearview mirror and stared at the odd little man who was still standing beside the road—though now a few steps farther back—with his thumb in the air. He glanced in their direction and then away, as if trying not to look like he was staring.

"It's so hot outside," the wife said without a hint of sarcasm in her voice. Her husband glanced over to her and saw the worry lines creased between her eyes. "And he's still twenty miles away from town, at least."

"He kinda looks like a leprechaun," the man said.

"Don't be like that..." She tilted her head a bit, still staring in the rearview. "Oh, actually, yeah. I see it." She put the car in reverse and started rolling back toward the man.

"Wait, no! What are you doing?!"

"Even if he *is* a leprechaun, it's too hot to be out today."

"I'm not worried about him being a leprechaun, babe. I'm worried about him being a serial killer!"

"He could die out here."

"*We* could die out here!"

"*Pfft*. You're so dramatic." The wife waved away his concern with a brush of her hand and an eye roll. She grinned when her husband realized he couldn't change her mind. "Driver chooses the stops." She winked.

The car stopped, and the husband studied the ragged hitchhiker while rolling down the window. He looked a bit like a Toll House elf who became human-sized and was trying to figure out how to blend in. He was a little on the shortish side, with ears that were a little on the longish side, and his springy gray hair was slicked back in a red bandanna. An odd assortment of clothes completed the ensemble, as if he had scrounged together whatever he could find to cover himself.

"Where you headed?" The wife asked.

"Oh, just wherever you're a-goin'," he said jovially, flashing a cheerful grin.

At hearing the Irish accent, the husband turned to his wife with raised eyebrows and mouthed the word *Leprechaun*.

She elbowed him as she leaned closer to the window. "Well, we can certainly drop you off in the next town. We have water bottles and granola bars in the back seat. Help yourself to whatever you need."

The man beamed. "Well, thank ye kindly, both!"

He tossed his duffel bag into the back seat and slid in with it. The wife tried not to cringe at the smell rising up from the man's dusty bare feet. The hitchhiker made himself comfortable, stretching out and asking the husband if he wouldn't mind moving his seat up a "wee bit" so he could have some extra legroom. The husband, who was very tall, grunted but pulled his seat forward for the much shorter man. He glared at his wife. She rolled her eyes and shot a "be nice" look back at him.

"What are you doing out here in the desert?" The husband asked the hitchhiker in an attempt to appease his wife. He glanced at the rearview mirror. The passenger was staring out the window, watching the arid landscape with an odd grin on his face. He did not answer the question. The husband asked, a little louder this time, how the hitchhiker had come to find himself in the middle of nowhere.

Instead of responding, the hitchhiker leaned forward and peered around the seat. "I like your shoes," the barefoot man said, pressing much too closely into the husband's personal space.

"Thank you," the husband replied un-comfortably. He shifted a bit in his seat and glanced down at his brown leather loafers.

"I think you could walk a good distance in shoes like those."

"Yeah... I wear these a lot," he said, trying to think of a way out of the conversation.

Changing the subject, his wife asked, "Where are you from, originally?"

She watched her husband let out a relieved breath. He

continued to fix his stare on every sign they passed as if their lives depended on his reading and rereading the *Speed Limit 55* and *Pass With Care* notices.

"Well, I'm a bit from everywhere," the man said with a chuckle. "But originally from the beautiful woodlands of Ireland." His face held a wistful expression, as though he was looking out at the desert but picturing the lush green hills of his country.

"You're a long way from home."

"Aye." He said nothing more.

"How did you find yourself here?"

"I came for a visit..." A shadow passed over his face, and his voice quieted and took on a bitter grit. "My stay was...extended." He drew out the final word as if it left a bad taste in his mouth. It was a heavy word. It held some story but also seemed to warn against further pressing for answers.

Something in the man's change of tone made the woman's throat go dry, and a little chill ran across her shoulders. She stopped asking questions and reached over to the water bottle in her cup holder. The next time she glanced back at him in the rearview mirror he met her eye and flashed a disarming grin. Surely it had been nothing.

The silence stretched on a few more moments until the hitchhiker filled it by helping himself to the box of road trip snacks in the back seat. The husband flipped on the radio to distract himself from the sounds of the stranger's grubby hands rummaging through the bag of his favorite chips that he'd brought for the long drive. Again, he was met with static.

"We sure are isolated," the man said between mouthfuls of chips. "I'll bet even the phones don't work this far out of town." He stuffed the empty chips bag back into the box of snacks and began to voraciously chug bottles of water and eat one granola bar after another.

The husband glanced down at the cell phone in his lap. No bars. No data. He looked at his wife. Her face was a bit more tense than before, but she didn't look truly concerned.

He was startled when the hitchhiker shot forward, his face suddenly directly between the couple, staring down at the husband's feet.

"I *really* like those shoes," he said.

"Please sit down," said the husband, pressing his fingertips into his forehead.

The hitchhiker sat back in his seat but continued talking about the shoes. "I figure we wear about the same size, wouldn't you think?" He propped one bare foot up on the center console.

The husband looked like he was about to have an aneurysm. His jaw was clenched, his face bright red, his hand balled into a fist, and he was looking out the window with such concentrated irritation that his wife wondered, with amusement, whether he was trying to shatter the glass with his stare. The buildings in the distance were larger now, stretching out in a series of long compounds.

"I'm a cobbler by trade. I could make you a nicer pair than that," the hitchhiker continued, not seeming to notice the husband's very focused attempts to ignore him. "It'll be grand: if you give me those shoes on your feet now, when I get back home to my workshop, I'll—"

"I am NOT going to give you my shoes!" The words erupted from his mouth with such intensity that the hitchhiker actually stopped his rambling and sat silently for a long moment.

No one spoke.

The three passed a mile or two in silence. The wife considered trying to change the subject again, but decided to let the moment pass. She scanned the landscape, which now was partly blocked out by the unmarked, fenced-in buildings. Warehouses, maybe? Her eyes fell on a worn white sign coming up on their right, which she registered as being unlike usual traffic signs. She started to read the words with a bored curiosity, then froze. A flood of dread washed over her. Her husband reached across and grabbed her hand, and she realized that he'd just read it too.

DO NOT PICK UP HITCHHIKERS

PRISON AHEAD

All the oxygen was sucked out of the cramped car. The wife could feel her heartbeat pounding in her ears, and beside her, her husband's breathing had grown ragged and heavy. The silence was so thick that it felt as though there was a literal weight on her rigid shoulders. Shock and panic ran in waves up her spine as she glanced at another sign coming up on their right at the entrance of the chain-link fence.

PENITENTIARY OF NEW MEXICO

She could feel the stranger's eyes on the back of her neck as they passed the sign and then passed the buildings, which she now knew were *not* warehouses. Her husband's hand gripped hers tightly as the penitentiary compound faded behind them.

Maybe it was a coincidence. It could've been a coincidence...

The woman took a deep breath, worked up all the courage in her trembling body, and without turning her head, glanced up to the right to look at the stranger in the rearview mirror. Her eyes met his icy, unflinching stare. The last of her hope drained from her pale face. She glanced at her husband, whose eyes were squeezed shut, his lips blanched and pressed tightly together, as if he was trying to take back the angry outburst from ten minutes earlier that had most likely sealed their fates.

The stranger leaned forward in his seat again. The wife shuddered at his nearness, and her husband's panicked breathing grew louder. Very calmly, slowly, the stranger said, "I think you should give me your shoes now."

In numb, clumsy movements, the husband reached down to take off his shoes. "You can have my watch too," he said, his voice breaking between the words. All of the confidence and authority was gone, and now thick, panicked desperation took its place. "We don't have a lot of cash, but you can have all of it."

He put the shoes carefully on the center console and kept his hands in the air where the stranger could see them.

"And...and jewelry. You can have my wife's jewelry...anything you want...just, please..." He couldn't finish the sentence. His face was screwed up, and his wife knew that he would start weeping if he said another word.

"We'll give you the car if you let us out safely," she said, fighting to keep her voice steady. She glanced in the mirror again to see whether her words had landed.

The stranger was still tying up the laces. He took a long moment to consider, and she was afraid her voice had been too weak the first time and he hadn't heard her. She was fighting up the courage to repeat herself when the man glanced up.

"No. Just the shoes."

He looked with satisfaction at his feet. Apparently, they did fit after all.

The woman's hands were gripping the steering wheel so tightly that her knuckles had gone ghostly white. A single tear rolled silently down her face, but she didn't dare reach up to wipe it away. In her peripheral vision, she saw her husband's hand move a few inches toward hers, and she reached out to grasp it.

They were going to die. No one would know where their bodies were hidden. They were going to be murdered in the middle of this desert, their bodies tossed into a shallow grave, and all anyone would ever know was that they'd gone missing on a road trip.

They were going to die.

Her mind, numb with shock and horror, tried to accept the fact. It couldn't.

She held tightly to her husband's hand and tried, without breaking the thick silence, to communicate her love for him in that one touch. She felt the wedding band on his finger. There was something comforting in the solidness of it. He slid his fingers between hers, and she took a deep breath.

The penitentiary was miles behind them now, and it had been too long since they'd seen another vehicle.

"Turn off the highway up ahead there," said the gruff voice from the back seat.

The woman kept driving.

"I said *slow the car* and *take the turn.*"

She heard a click, and in the side of her vision saw the black metallic gleam of a gun being pointed at the back of her husband's head.

She began to turn to see better, but the man snapped at her sharply, "Eyes on the road!"

She quickly looked away from him, then squeezed her beloved's hand tighter, almost apologetically, and obeyed the stranger's instructions until they were at least two miles off Route 14.

"Now. Pull over."

The vehicle jolted with a finality, like a death sentence, when she shifted it into park. She swallowed, but her throat was so dry and closed that she felt like she was silently choking.

There was a rustling sound, like snacks being stuffed

into a duffel bag, but the wife didn't dare turn her head again. She heard the stranger shift the sack onto his shoulder and unclick his seatbelt.

"Get out of the car. Very slowly." The thickly accented voice was like dripping syrup. Slow and heavy and poisonous.

"You don't have to do this," the husband said. "We never saw you. We won't say a thing. We just want to get home and go back to our boring lives. I swear, we don't care what you do with the car, just let us out and keep on driving."

He continued to ramble as he and his wife got out of the vehicle and stepped into the suffocating heat. They kept their arms up in the air, careful not to turn their heads and look directly at the man with the gun. Following instructions, they put their hands on the burning hot hood of the car. Sand bunched beneath the husband's socks. The sun beat mercilessly down on their heads. Their hands found each other again.

"Please," the husband begged. "Just let my wife go. That's all I'm asking, just let *her* leave—"

"Quiet!" snapped the man. "*Now*, I want you to ask me what I did with the gold."

"What?" The husband looked back, confused, but the stranger yelled at him to face forward, and he whipped his head back to the windshield compliantly.

"Ask me where I hid my gold."

"Okay, okay." The husband took a deep breath, wondering what sadistic game he was playing along with and whether this was going to be the last sentence he ever spoke. He held his wife's hand like it was the first time and realized that here, at the end of his life, his only wish was for more moments with her.

"Where..." he started. He took one more breath, working up his strength, squeezed his eyes shut, and said, "Where did you hide the gold?"

A loud sound exploded behind them, which he realized a half-second later was not a gunshot, but an eruption of laughter.

The little man howled with rumbling, belly-aching cackles.

"Ye should have seen your faces!" He screamed the words into the sky.

Then, with shocking suddenness, the sound stopped. The silence stretched on for a full minute before the husband turned around in confusion. The hitchhiker was gone. There were no footprints, no duffel bag, no gun, no snacks, no shoes. The only evidence that he had been there at all was a black stapler dropped in the sand where the gun should have been.

"What just happened?" the husband asked when he was able to speak again. His wife just stared in shock.

They did not finish their vacation.

Three weeks later, when the confused couple had returned home and happily resumed their normal lives, a shoebox-sized package arrived on their doorstep, postmarked from an address in Carlingford, County Louth, Ireland. Inside was a little note the size of a business card sticking out of a beautifully crafted, brand-new pair of brown loafers.

Thanks for the laugh, read the note. *Here are the shoes, as promised. Best o' luck to you both.*
Your Friend,
The Leprechaun

Scaredy Cat on Halloween Night
by Effie Joe Stock

Darkness creeped
As I lay asleep,
Dreams quickly turning
To nightmares unfurling
And things that go bump in the night.

A noise I heard,
Like a dying bird,
Startling me from sleep,
The stairs creaked
As the nightmares came to life.

Huddled in fear
Waiting to hear
What could it be?
What was coming for me,
In the air now cold with fright?

Effie Joe Stock

Wind howling,
Shutters clattering
Branches moaning
Hinges creaking.
Will everything end tonight?

The door opens,
My heart beats broken
In the door of my room
A figure looms.
I wait for its cold bite.

Streaming from eyes shut tight
Tears I'm afraid to wipe
From cheeks buried
Under covers where I scurried
To hide from the shadows of the night.

Hands grabbing!
Teeth gnawing!
I scream and flail
But to no avail
My life will end in fight.

But now there is laughter!

Scaredy Cat on Halloween Night

Covers thrown back; my fear is shattered.
Casting off an old sheet,
Leaps my brother to his feet,
"Scaredy cat!" he mocks my plight

Cheeks red,
I leap from my bed
Tackling him to the ground
Feeling like a clown
How scared I had been this Halloween night!

Humble Pie

by Kristiana Sfirlea

I found a pumpkin in a patch
All the squash around it smashed
The slimy guts and chunks of orange
And prints where furry creatures foraged
All enclosed that lone survivor
Poor thing had been through something dire

I took the pumpkin home with me
I had a plan for it, you see
To win the first-place ribbon
Of the pumpkin competition

I tucked the pumpkin into bed
And patted it on its orange head
"Tomorrow is All Hallows Eve.
I'll win that prize, or I'll be peeved.
My picking skills know no match.

Kristiana Sfirlea

You'll be glad you left your patch."

I really was the very best
With me around, there's no contest
That first-place ribbon would be mine
I'd show them all, no need to be kind

And so I went to bed myself
And put my daydreams on a shelf
I didn't think another word
Until the screaming sound was heard
"Something's smashed them," cried the town.
"There's not a pumpkin to be found."

I rushed into my pumpkin's room
Afraid that it had met its doom
But there it sat, all sound and safe
The pumpkin slaughter it had escaped

"I have one here," I told the town proudly.
"This means I win, I'm convinced most devoutly."
"Wait!" rose a voice, tender and small
And out came a girl only four feet tall
The pumpkin she held was just as petite
A beautiful thing, tiny and sweet

Humble Pie

I hugged my pumpkin in my arms
Mine was bigger but hers had more charm
She was sure to win the ribbon
I had to eliminate my competition

Suddenly, with a giant bound
My precious pumpkin hit the ground
It hopped with supernatural force
Towards girl and gourd, it set its course
And knocked the pumpkin from her grasp
Pounded it to pulp just as fast

I watched the scene with great dismay
I didn't want to win this way
A girl crying, a pummeled friend
The evil pumpkin couldn't win in the end

"You're just like my pride, fiendish and strong!
I see now that I have been wrong."
And with these words, I swung my fists
Smashing the pumpkin into bits
I took home the pieces—I had a new plan
I needed flour, sugar, and a pan

All the apologies I had to make
I poured in a bowl and began to bake
I finished at dawn, the sun in the sky
And everyone feasted on humble pie

Part Three:
In the Dread of Night

The Night Walkers
by Emily Barnett

The sun had barely risen, but we were already behind.

I watched as Father cracked open the cabin door and stood still, listening. His breath made white puffs of clouds against the dark woods beyond. Through the window I saw light slipping over the horizon, and a grey-blue began to hem up the sky, the stars becoming lost in the backdrop. A bird sang into the silence with one sweet, timid note as if it didn't want to be caught.

I shivered in my nest of animal furs and wool blankets. At some point, the fire had turned to embers. The cold had crept in quickly. But I remained still, in case what hid in the shadows was still out there, lurking. Listening.

"All right," Father whispered. "It's safe."

Without fear of being heard, my older brother, Douglas, slid on his boots and stomped around the cabin to regain blood flow.

"Hurry up, little star," Father said, nodding to me. I slid behind the curtain to clothe myself in as many layers as I could. The chill still clung.

Douglas and I entered the land of white. We waded through the snow as if we were sloshing through water. I wished it was summer when night and snow didn't own the world. Now, it felt as if both time and the elements were against us.

The sun was directly above our heads when we reached the river. The small streams near our home were too frozen to break through—either from the cruelty of nature or a consequence of our cursed land—so we made the trip to the big river for water, and fish, if we were lucky. Even cursed lands contained luck sometimes.

But it wasn't fish we caught that day.

A woman stood on the riverbank, staring across the rushing water.

I called out a greeting, and she turned in surprise. Douglas glared warily under his leather hood, but I thought her face looked trustworthy. Father said I had a knack for that sort of thing.

"I'm Ava, and this is Douglas," I said, stepping forward.

"Claire," she offered. "I'm trying to make my way to the towns."

My stomach tightened as Douglas and I shared a look.

The shortest way to the West towns was through our land on a single road cutting through forest and nightmare. Most traveled around, though it added days to their excursion. Those we caught passing through were either running from their own ghosts—or were fools.

"You won't make it today," he said shortly. "You can stay with us for the night, then depart at first light."

Claire looked at us suspiciously. It was hard to tell how old she was under her layers of fabric, but her hair was raven black, and her brown eyes appeared youthful.

"You mustn't be in the woods after sundown," I said, hoping to assuage her, but it only seemed to deepen her wariness. After hesitating for a few more seconds, she sighed, then nodded. Perhaps the curse of our land—the Dark Lands—was well-known. I had never been to the towns, so I didn't know.

Douglas and I lowered some lines in the water, but after an hour, we still hadn't caught a thing. As I was pulling mine up, I heard a *snap* near the tree line. I turned sharply, staring into the dark boughs. Surely, we weren't in danger yet. But the longer I stared, the more uneasy I felt. Something was watching us.

"I think we should head back," I whispered.

Douglas nodded, tucking the lines in his bag, then

grabbing two of the water-filled pails. He never questioned my intuition about the things that lurked in the darkness. Maybe I had a knack for that too.

Claire took a bucket from me, and we turned, following our own footprints—the only blemishes in the porcelain landscape.

"Why don't you melt snow for water?" Claire asked as we grew closer to our cabin. The buckets of sloshing water only added to our misery. I was already dreaming of a warm fire and Father's deep voice lulling us to sleep with his songs.

"The big river flows from the Light Lands," Douglas said between strained breaths. "The snow and what sleeps under the trees are not safe."

She looked up sharply. "Don't *you* sleep under them?"

"Our home is made with lumber from the Light Lands," I said. "It protects us."

Claire's forehead wrinkled. "Why do you live here if it's so dangerous?"

Douglas' hand slipped, and water sloshed over the side of his pail. "We're the guardians," he said gruffly. "If we hadn't been here, you'd be dead."

Claire didn't ask any more questions.

I understood my brother's frustration, though it didn't flow as bitterly in my veins. Douglas would inherit the burden. One day, I would be free from it. I had once asked

Father why we didn't sell the land. He said that even if we could find a naïve buyer, he wouldn't. Father was merciful enough to know they wouldn't last one night. Our family knew every trick to survive, every inch of this place. We couldn't break the ancient curse, but we could keep it from breaking us.

It was late afternoon by the time we reached the cabin, and already the sun was descending. But we were prepared. It was the Winter Solstice, the longest night of the year. And unfortunately for us, the shortest day.

Father emerged from the cabin; a faint smell of smoky leaves stuck in the fibers of his shirt. Claire and Father introduced themselves.

"Come, warm yourself. It's going to be a long night."

Douglas and I set about pouring the river water into small pots around the outside of the cabin. Father lit the sticks and coal underneath them.

"The water isn't for drinking?" Claire asked.

"Some," Father said, nodding. "But this is for the Walkers. They are deterred by the scent and shouldn't bother us."

I raised a brow at Douglas, who shook his head. Father obviously didn't want to frighten Claire. However, the kinder thing might have been to warn her that the Night Walkers were *much* more persistent on the Winter Solstice.

Glancing across the yard, I noticed that the forest's shadows were now caressing the edge of the cabin. The birds had gone silent. The fading sunlight soaked into the snow, giving it a deep red glow. *Warning. Warning,* nature seemed to say.

"Father?" I whispered, tugging at his coat.

"Inside," he said.

Once the door was shut, it was a flurry of motion. Claire sat on the bed watching with interest as we moved in a synchronized dance of lighting candles and laying stones with markings at the bottom of the door. I retrieved a teapot of boiling river water from the fireplace, poured it into a large mortar, and with a pestle, ground-up dried leaves and dirt from the Light Lands, until it became a thick mush.

"Should've done that sooner, little star," Father said with warning. "Hurry now." Goosebumps danced up my skin. "All done," I said shakily, handing him the bowl.

With quick, strong movements, he used a horsehair brush to paint the door and window frames, all while praying protection over our small cabin. I uttered my own prayer. It didn't matter that I had been through thirteen years of dark nights. Fear never lost its bite.

No sooner had Father finished with the door than we heard a long, far-off shriek.

The quiet that followed was even louder.

"What was that?" Claire whispered. She had shed her mound of cloaks and scarves, and I could now see she was no older than Douglas. Even though there were dark circles under her eyes, she was quite pretty. Douglas seemed to notice as well.

"The Night Walkers," he said with a gentler tone.

"But what *are* they? I've only heard stories..." she shook her head as if trying to recall them. Most people we met crossing our land didn't take our warnings seriously, thinking they were folk tales to scare children.

Those were the people we found in the early morning light, either drowned or speared by their own weapons or frozen, staring glassy-eyed at the horizon as if they'd been waiting for the sun.

Father cleared his throat. "We believe the Walkers are formless, taking on the nightmares of whoever sees them," he threw another log on the fire. "Come, get warm."

We obeyed. I was anxious to turn my back to the window. I didn't know what would be worse: meeting my deepest fear or always wondering what it was. Was it death or something else? Would the Walkers show me our home, the place I felt most safe, and the place that, sometimes, felt like a suffocating grave?

The fire crackled pleasantly, and I leaned into its warmth and brightness. My thoughts filled with the sun and what the Light Lands—a place with no night—must be like. Even the towns brought hope to my chilled frame. Not many had reached the Light Lands, but the Mid Lands made up most of the world. The Mid Landers were normal, happy people. Or so I assumed. I studied Claire. She tucked a strand of raven hair behind an ear, and I glimpsed a bruise on her neck.

"What—" I began.

Bang. Bang. Bang.

My breath stilled.

Claire shrieked and latched onto Douglas' arm.

Father's knuckles turned white as he gripped his knees.

Bang. Bang. Bang.

The Walkers had come.

Winter Solstice drove them mad. Made them bold. They knew the sun would take longer to reach them.

A low moan, like wind through a cracked window, swirled around the room. Douglas squeezed Claire close to him to stop her shaking.

There was a scratch, a single scratching fingernail, that slid down the wood door. I swallowed hard. Though formless, as Father claimed, they could still, somehow, create noise. The noise was the worst part.

Another bang.

Our breaths were too loud, but it didn't matter. They

knew we were here.

The handle began to rattle, as if something was trying to unlock the door. I gasped at the Night Walker's boldness, and before I could stop myself, I turned.

My eye caught something white through the keyhole.

It blinked.

Then it laughed.

"Ava!" Father said, grabbing my face and cradling it safely into his chest. He wrapped his big, bear arms around me. But I still shivered. Had it seen me?

"Aaaava," came a woman's sing-song voice, muffled by the door.

My Father's grip stiffened, and Douglas' tan face lost its color.

"Why did you do it, Aaaava?"

A knot of dread pushed up through my stomach so violently I thought I would vomit. I should have named this fear before it called to me. I should've known. It had shackled itself to my twiggy legs since birth, no matter how I tried to ignore it.

Douglas reached for the candle on the table and dripped wax into a bowl. Even though his color hadn't returned, his good sense had. He began molding the wax until they would fit snugly into our ears.

The hinges of the door creaked under another round of

violent pounding and scratching. Claire was crying. Father's arms trembled around me.

"Here," Douglas said, shoving two into my palm.

But before I could act, the noise ceased, and the voice whispered into the ringing silence. "Why did you kill me, Aaaava?"

I cried out as if the Walker had yelled, and I hastily shoved the warm wax into my ears. Father held me so tight it hurt.

The knot in my throat burst open, and with shoulders heaving and breath catching, I sobbed into his chest. He rubbed my hair and hummed a tune from my mother's childhood; I could feel the rhythm. Its familiar sound brought warmth to my limbs.

Not just warmth—a blaze. As my fear and self-loathing rose, so did the fire within me.

A burning sensation was filling my ribs, my lungs, my fingertips. Father pulled back, or maybe I pulled away from him. I felt feverish. Weak yet powerful at the same time.

What was happening?

"Father?" I whispered.

The candles suddenly flared, the fire in the hearth grew bright, embers sparking dangerously into the room. Douglas and Father bounded to their feet, tamping down the flames before they consumed the entire cabin.

The Night Walker shrieked then fled. Somehow, I knew it had fled.

Then, I was falling into darkness, into cold.

Into sleep.

I dreamt of my mother. That is, I dreamt of what I *thought* my mother looked like based on Father's sketches and descriptions from Douglas. Though they never said so, in my dreams, her face always shone brightly. Like a star.

When I woke, her glow was still warm on my eyelids.

I blinked.

It was only sunlight. *Morning.* We had made it.

I blew out a relieved breath and glanced around. The cabin was quiet, but a normal quiet, not one born out of fear. Father was gone, most likely outside, checking the perimeter. Douglas slept soundly in his bed.

A creak on the floorboards told me Claire was awake, and I sat up to find her by the window. "You haven't left?" I asked. She needed to go soon if she had any hope of making it.

She shook her head.

I scrambled to my feet and stood beside Claire at the window. I sucked in a breath when I saw what she was looking at—a woman's handprint outlined by the frosted glass. Little by little, it began to disappear, as if it had been waiting for me to see. To remind me that it had been here.

"Your mother died in childbirth?" Claire asked, tearing her eyes from the glass.

I pulled my sweater tighter around me and nodded. My first breath had taken her last.

Claire gave me an even gaze—no sympathy, no blame. "Can I tell you a secret, Ava?" she whispered, ducking her head to meet my level. "It isn't just your land that is cursed." I glimpsed the bruise on her neck again. Her eyes glistened even as they hardened. "Nightmares that haunt us, that hurt us...they come in many forms. From many places."

I shook my head stubbornly. "Not in the Light Lands."

Claire studied me for a moment, then smiled. "Perhaps not," she said with a sigh, straightening to look out the window again. "It's a nice thought."

The dread from the Night Walker clung to me even as the handprint faded. And now, Claire's words echoed through my mind, only adding to my misery. *Was the world truly so bleak?* And the bigger question—the one that spilled out in the late hours when day seemed so far—could I ever be good enough to glimpse those lands where the sun always shone?

Leaving Claire by the window, I bundled against the cold and went looking for Father. At the edge of the dark forest, I found him chopping firewood from our leftover trees we kept in the shed. The sun glinted off his axe with each swing, and I leaned into the familiar sound. A normal, rhythmic sound. Father straightened and rubbed his lower back, eyeing me as I stood silently by.

"It was a lie, little star," Father said. I cocked my head. "Walkers only see our fears and call them out," he continued. "And fear skews truth."

"So, she didn't..." I swallowed. The frozen morning air was dry in my throat.

"Your mother died, but *you* did not stop her breath. It was her body. Her time," he said firmly. "If you think you're not worth it, then I have lost you both." He gathered an arm full of wood and began to lug it home. The knot within my chest didn't fully unravel, but I felt a few chords tug free.

"Where did you meet?" I asked his retreating form. He paused, so I continued. "I dream of Mother almost every night," I whispered. "And her face is always glowing." It felt foolish saying it out loud, like a child's ramblings. But the wood dropped from Father's hands, falling deep into the snow with a soft thud. He turned.

"Glows?"

I nodded.

He strode back to me, taking my face into his cold hands, studying me deeply as if I were a newborn, and he was memorizing every line of my face, every freckle, every speck of gold in my green eyes.

"It might be time you knew." His voice caught.

"Knew what?"

"Your mother. She was born of the Light Lands." His words were quiet, but they struck me so deeply I took a dizzying step back.

"She was—?"

He nodded, smiling. "She had sun magic."

It was impossible. Wonderful. Yet deep down, I felt as if I'd always known. My mother's homeland had been calling to me as if it had a claim on my soul.

"You have the same magic in your veins, Ava."

"The fire," I whispered, thinking on last night and how the flames had seemed to burn out of my very chest.

"The fire, yes. And your uncanny way of sensing the Walkers." Father's eyes gleamed. "And how your magic has protected us these past thirteen years."

"*What*?"

"All the precautions: the river water, the symbols at the door...they are only backups. It's *you* that both attracts and repels the Walkers."

"Me?"

Father nodded.

Sun magic. It was amazing, and it might have been enough to cover our cabin, but could a single ray do anything against an entire land of nightmares?

I'd be devoured.

I told Father as much, but he shook his head.

"Do you know why I never lose hope when the Winter Solstice nears?"

I shrugged.

"Because I know the sun will push back the night a little more each day after." He hugged me tight to his chest and whispered into my yellow hair. "And that's what we'll do, little star. We'll keep pushing back the night. Day by day."

Bleached Reminders
by Effie Joe Stock

Speak softly of death, they say
Death looms closer, not so far away.
But I wonder,
Why are we filled with dismay?

Perhaps we're afraid to be forgotten
Afraid our memories will be broken
But we all leave something behind,
Waiting for stories to be spoken.

When all has rotted away,
Pieces of our bodies scattered array,
Bones remain—
The frame that held us straight

Cleaned by nature, free of blight
Kissed by the sun and bleached clean white

Pure reminders
Of lives that dimmed with fight.

Gather the bones of the dead to you,
Hold them tenderly and remember their value
And listen gently
To what they leave in residue.

"I lived. I lived. I lived."
They cry. Their words, once adrift,
Now whisper to you,
Reminding you why you exist,

And how you will not be forgotten,
When you at last taste death's kiss.

Possession
by L.A. Thornhill

It was not vanity or childish ambition that led me to ask my father for a quarter of my inheritance to travel the world. No, it was what I believed to be a pursuit of wisdom and experience. I had finished my first year at the university and found myself unsatisfied. I studied the world around me but had not seen or tasted any of it. This lack of experience convinced me that a year off from my studies to travel was just what I needed to truly be educated.

My father, an aged and kind man, hesitated at my request. "Did we not agree that your travel would come after graduation?"

I had prepared for such an inquiry, having thought on this venture for an entire semester. "But this is the year of Uthatica's three-hundredth independence anniversary. It is said that it will be the festival of a lifetime. Not to mention the races of Duskhaven will take place at the end of the year, and—"

My father lifted his hand, silencing me. "So many wondrous things happening only this year, eh?"

"Perhaps not all are *only* this year, Father, but what a year it shall be!"

He stroked his chin. His thin white beard was neatly trimmed, but his eyebrows could use the same care. "I do not advise this, Allan. You are still young and have seen little beyond our country. I fear what others might devise when they learn your name."

"Not to worry. I have decided to take on my mother's name. I will be merely Allan Latimer, student on leave, not Allan Zadock, heir to the Zadock estate and title."

Father sighed. "I see your heart is set on this journey, and you have never troubled your mother and me like so many other youths have their parents. Very well." He pressed a small brown button on his desk. "Maxwell, please enter the study."

"As you wish, Lord Zadock," a voice vibrated from the speaker next to the button.

A whirring echoed in the hall before the door opened, revealing Maxwell, father's automaton butler: a lean bot in a body of polished copper with three metal wagon wheels for mobility. His head was round with two pale blue lights for eyes and a speaker for a mouth. Two arms with anatomically correct hands gestured as he spoke. "How may

I serve your lordship?"

"Make an appointment with my banker on the morrow," Father ordered.

"As you wish." The automation rolled backward out of the room.

With a light heart, I knelt at my father's side. "I cannot thank you enough."

Father would not meet my gaze. "You have always been a good son. Promise me you will remain just that for your mother and me."

"Of course, Father."

"Promise me, Allan."

I laid my hand on his. "I give you my word. I only wish to travel and learn, Father. That's why I am only asking for a quarter of my inheritance. It should allow me to travel comfortably but not lavishly."

Father snorted. "You have not learned to discern the difference."

"But I will now."

"Must you go alone?" Father asked.

I nodded. "Aye, I must. I want my independence."

"It is not your independence that I wish to deprive you of. What concerns me are the dangers that a young man of fortune might be dealt due to his ignorance."

"I wish for this journey to remove my ignorance. Trust

me."

Father took my hand. "I choose to trust you."

The following morning, Father bestowed me a parcel with the promised amount. In less than an hour, I was packed and sending Maxwell out to prepare the carriage. I had no time to waste. If I left now, I could return in exactly one year and be prepared for university life once more.

Father accompanied me to the train station where I procured my first ticket with my newly acquired inheritance. Mother remained behind at the estate, weeping as if I had passed away from some sudden illness. Perhaps to her, I had. But the illness that drove me to venture beyond the border of the country that I had known so intimately for nineteen years was intoxicating.

I shook Father's hand on the steps of my compartment. He forced a smile, but his eyes betrayed his dread.

"Any advice, Father?" I asked as the train whistled.

"Choose your friends wisely."

I gave him my best reassuring smile. "Trust me."

For the next three months, I kept my vow as if my parents were accompanying me. I was their son in action, if not in name, on my travels. But oh, how I loved the travels.

Though alone, I never ceased long enough to be lonely. I toured cities, climbed majestic, ruined castles, and ate local delicacies. If there was one indulgence that I permitted myself, it was that of food.

It was this very indulgence that brought me into the company of Professor Thavian Darknoll.

I arrived in the country of Uthatica and lost myself in the wild, exuberant celebration of the citizens' liberty. I danced with every pretty girl who would accept my hand until my feet and stomach ached. The latter I remedied with a reservation at the finest restaurant the country boasted.

However, my reservation was lost and my table taken. Furious, I demanded another table. To which the host, a bald, paunch man whose self-importance was higher than his height, smirked and dismissed me with a wave of the hand.

I might have accepted defeat if I wasn't famished from dancing.

Without thought, I whipped out my passport, revealing my true identity and the significance of the insult. As the Zadock heir, I fully comprehended the influence my father held. His name was known, his reputation as a politician and lord transcended borders. And for tonight, it overcame a lost reservation.

Apologies were made, and an automaton waiter—slightly less polished than Maxwell back home—seated me at a balcony table. I smiled with triumph at my improved circumstances.

A clear, star-filled night welcomed me. Fireworks danced on the horizon with greater skill than I had. The city was vibrant with lights and colors of the festivities, and I watched with great zeal at the happy citizens beneath me.

The automaton returned, this time with a menu in hand, and asked me a question in the Uthatican tongue, to which I was significantly deficient.

"Language change, if you please," I said.

There was a clicking inside the automaton and its eyes dimmed for a few seconds, then resumed their brightness, and said, "Language change complete. How might I serve you, good sir?"

I ordered a steak, vegetables, and a glass of wine. I also ordered a dessert, wanting it to be ready as soon as the last bite of steak was devoured.

"Excellent, sir." The bot removed the menu from the table. "One more thing. A patron at another table requested to join you."

I blinked, surprised by the request. "Who?"

The automaton motioned the menu towards a table across the room, the very table that had been stolen from me. I was predisposed to deny the request, still irritated at the loss, when my eyes fell upon the man there.

He appeared to be in his mid-forties, slicked-back hair, small glasses, with a trim beard. He wore fine attire, a three-piece suit of jade and a black waistcoat. But it was the enormous book open at the table that caught my eye. It was an old and well-read tome, judging by the frayed leather binding that I could see even from here.

What sort of man brings a tome to a restaurant? Curiosity compelled me to accept the request, but I'm ashamed to say my pride was still sufficiently injured. I politely declined to the bot.

I had just convinced myself to forget the offer while enjoying my appetizer when the tome settled next to my plate with a thud. I looked up and came face-to-face with the man. He gave the confident smile of a man who fully comprehended his skills in a social situation.

"Good evening, Mr. Latimer," the man's fierce grey eyes bore into me from beyond the spectacles. "Forgive my intrusion, but I believe it would be a great disservice to other guests if two tables were taken by two men when we could share one."

It was one thing to reject the offer to a metal servant; it

was another to reject the man. I nodded and motioned for him to take the seat opposite me.

"Professor Thavian Darknoll at your service," he said, flipping his coattails back as he sat. "Was our waiter correct in referring to you as Latimer?"

I swallowed, relieved that my true name had been kept from the automaton. So the host did one thing right. "Correct. Allan Latimer."

The waiter brought over his salad and drink and made a quick comment about the professor's meal being brought to this table shortly. The professor waved him off without facing the automaton.

"An old scholar with a book might be expected to be alone at a restaurant, but a young man such as yourself? I am perplexed."

I shrugged. "I had been dancing before I arrived. None of the young ladies wanted to leave the festivities, not even for a meal." I coughed. "I suspect they preferred the other men who are much more proficient on their feet than I."

We chatted inanely for a few minutes, and I started to dread the idea of passing my meal in such a manner. Until my eyes fell upon the tome once more. The title arrested my attention.

"*The Unnatural History of Death*," I read aloud. "By Dr. Emory Osgood." I raised an eyebrow at the professor.

"Forgive me, but what could possibly be unnatural about death? It seems to be the most natural thing in the world."

"Is it, though?" the professor inquired, pressing the tips of his fingers together as if thrilled by the question.

I was taken aback by his response. "Well... certainly. Everything dies eventually."

"And yet, throughout history, mankind has fought against death, whether using medicine, religion, or prestige. Why is it that man is so desperate to defeat the inevitable?"

I suspected Darknoll was asking me a rhetorical question, so I said nothing. My suspicion was quickly proven correct.

Darknoll scratched his temple, and I caught sight of a thin scar along his hairline. "Perhaps because, deep down, man isn't supposed to expire. We constantly learn. We should not cease to learn and contribute to the world. A world we have conquered."

"So death is the last thing to conquer?" I asked, trying to follow the professor's line of thinking.

"That is one way of looking at it, indeed." He took a sip of wine. "At least, that is what Dr. Osgood would have us believe. I am merely passing my time."

"And what is it that you teach, professor?"

"I'm retired, but I did specialize in Eastern World History. Though, I feel proficient enough to teach all of

World History, had I been given the time at universities."

"You seem awfully young to be retired."

Darknoll laughed a low, deep laugh. "I am older than I look, Allan—if I may refer to you by your first name."

I nodded.

"Don't be deceived by appearances," Darknoll continued, turning his head toward the city. "Take this country, for example—three hundred years of liberty, four hundred and seventy-two years of existence as Uthatica. And yet, how old is that for a country? It is but a youth compared to Atreland, Jupalor, and so forth. Still, much can be discovered in this young country. Far more enlightening and rich than anything you can find under those cheap lanterns that litter the city streets outside." He gestured toward the window.

The professor spoke with conviction, his voice thick like a priest with a burden. His eyes seemed to look past the celebrations to some ancient secret that I had no knowledge of. As I studied Darknoll, I realized that he was the type of man I *wanted* to be. Worldly, intelligent, and charming. If I were lucky, I could learn from this man and prove my father wrong.

"Forgive me," I said, "but is there any chance you could show me the history of this country?"

Darknoll smiled at me. "Of course."

After the meal, we made a plan to meet outside the restaurant tomorrow and then proceed to whatever historical destination the professor wanted to show me. He finished his dessert first, and then left, drawing the eyes of many attractive women in the restaurant.

I finished my meal and took his leave, drawing far less attention than my counterpart. A twinge of shame struck me, being outdone by a man at least thirty years my senior.

Yes, I wanted to be like him.

I did catch the attention of one man who was loitering outside the restaurant. Not exactly the company I wished to attract. He looked to be in his late thirties with thick mutton chops, a bowler hat and a tan coat and worn brown breeches. He approached me with his hands deep in his pockets.

"Excuse me, sir," he said, tipping his hat. "Took a wrong turn. Know the way to Fairfell Hotel?"

I had only been in the country for a few days, but I had passed the hotel in question on my way to the marketplace. "Take this road up a few blocks. It'll be on your left."

"Much thanks to you. Fellow tourist for the celebration?"

I nodded.

"Well, I suppose a Uthatican blessing is in order for

your help." He pressed his finger to his chin as if considering his words. "May your cupboards be full, your family warm, and may you choose your companions with caution."

I paused. "I believe the blessing ends with 'may your friends be wise.'"

"Maybe so." He rubbed the back of his neck. "Haven't quite mastered the Uthatican language. Anyway, good night."

I watched him go for about a block before I turned in the opposite direction to my own hotel.

Professor Thavian Darknoll did more than show me the history of Uthatica; we became travel companions for the next two months. He was on an extensive journey to celebrate his recent retirement.

Darknoll became a mentor to me. He had many odd and brilliant ideas of the world, all of which challenged and intrigued me as I had never known before. He had a seemingly immeasurable depth of knowledge. There wasn't a region we traveled to or a subject I spoke of that he didn't have some sort of information to contribute.

I learned that he was also skilled with his hands. On one occasion, I gave a letter to a post automaton to be delivered to my father. It was an older model of bot, possibly half a century old and rusted from long exposure to the elements. I slipped the letter into his chest cavity. The bot shuddered, and his gears grounded to a halt.

Instead of summoning an engineer, the professor removed a small pouch from inside his tailcoat and unraveled it. A set of small tools, all pristine, shone in the sunlight. He removed one thoughtfully and pried open the automaton. A few adjustments later, along with a scathing note to the local engineer about maintaining their automatons, he had the bot fixed.

"Is there nothing you can't do?" I asked, stunned at my friend's skill.

"Nothing that I have put effort into," he said calmly, wiping his tool down with a handkerchief.

"You haven't conquered death yet." I chuckled.

"Yes, that..." He replaced the tools in his coat. "All in good time, Allan."

After much travel, it was finally time for the Duskhaven races.

However, I had neglected my frugal methods of travel to keep up with Darknoll. I sailed on enormous steam liners instead of simple trains. I dined out often, for Darknoll favored good food as much as I did.

I was by no means poor or in danger of using up my quarter portion of inheritance. But if I didn't subside now, I would require assistance from my father before the end of the year. And as much as I wished to impress Darknoll, I wasn't about to seek more aid from my father.

I confessed all to Darknoll at dinner that night—yet another lavish restaurant. He still didn't know my true name, but he knew almost everything else about me; I trusted him completely, but my name was my only secret.

"My lad," he said, shaking his head at me. "You should have confided in me about this much sooner. How foolish to risk your money."

"I am not at risk," I said, feeling as chided as I had by my father. "I am merely concerned about the rest of my journey."

"As you should be. It was childish of you to use a piece of your inheritance in so frivolous a manner."

My face burned with embarrassment. "There is nothing frivolous about my journey. You of all people know my reasons and have complimented me on it."

"And you recall that I told you that this was a venture to undertake with your own earned money and not that of your father's."

Before I could defend myself, he waved a dismissive hand. "No matter. What's done is done. We will take the train next. No first class."

I frowned. "You do not have to sacrifice your comfort."

His eyes dropped to the last bite of salmon on his plate. His neck muscles were tight, and I noticed his skin colored. "I will ensure you are no longer wasteful, *Latimer*."

I was stunned at his anger at me and his use of my false last name. It was as if he were taking my frivolity personally.

The conversation changed to our usual discourse of history and culture.

Neither of us finished our meals.

The train Darknoll had chosen for us was an unusual one. It wasn't uncommon to see servant automatons on a train. However, this train, which had only two cars behind the engine, was entirely run by automatons. Not a man or woman in sight, not even as passengers. Darknoll explained that it was a small, experimental line that a relative of his ran.

Darknoll was in a most thoughtful manner, making notes in the margins of a new book, answering my inquiries with short replies. Two days into the train ride to

Duskhaven, Darknoll finally spoke to me.

We spoke of my family, as the train had brought back memories of the first day of my journey and the first real taste of homesickness I had felt. After knowing Darknoll as long as I had, I was comfortable in disclosing personal details I had withheld before. The subject focused primarily on my father and his opinions.

"My father is a politician. But he defies the stigma usually associated with men of that profession," I said, unable to disguise my pride in the fact. "He is a good, faithful man."

"Faithful?" Darknoll tilted his head. "Curious word choice. Religious man, is he?"

"Indeed. You will find him at the parish every Sunday."

"Doesn't mean he is religious. Many attend out of habit or cultural expectations."

"That is not my father."

Darknoll tapped the book in his hand. It was much smaller than the tome he had held when I first met him. "And what about you, Allan? In all the months we've been together, I've never known you to express a religious fancy."

I considered my reply, trying to balance what I felt and what he would respect. "I'm deciding for myself."

Darknoll nodded. "You have much to understand."

"What are your thoughts on religion?"

"One cannot ignore its impact on history." He gazed out the window, as thoughtful as he'd been the first night when he looked over Uthatica. "I am not a religious man myself. Much more driven by my studies than a deity. But even I cannot deny that the supposed 'Good Book' has had an...intellectual impact on me."

He scratched that same spot on his temple, disheveling his slick locks on the side, but made no attempt to straighten them out.

An hour later, the train came to a stop at a station. I peered out the window to see what appeared to be an abandoned town. No one walked the streets. Nearly every house and shop in view was filthy and had broken windows. A small platform served as a station.

Darknoll stood. "Come with me, Allan."

"Where are we?"

"Get up." Darknoll seized my arm and pulled me to my feet.

"I don't understand," I said as I stumbled out of the train car.

A carriage rode up, driven by an automaton. The horse, to my surprise, was also a full working automaton. I hadn't seen such metalwork before. The carriage was as dirty as the town, and the automatons had signs of rust.

Dread overtook me, and I refused to climb into the

carriage. But one of the automatons from the train pushed me inside. Darknoll sat on the seat opposite me. The automaton closed the door, and I heard it lock from the outside.

"I demand to know what is going on!" I shouted as the carriage lurched forward.

Darknoll scratched his head. "You'll know soon enou—"

"I want to know now!"

"Don't be so hasty, Zadock. It'll get you in trouble."

My blood froze. "You know."

"I didn't miss that little show you gave the host in Uthatica. I didn't know who exactly you were, but I figured it out in time. You're very forthcoming with your life. Most unwise."

I swallowed. "So this is a kidnapping."

"Nothing so vulgar." He glanced out the window. "We have arrived."

The carriage came to a stop, and I found myself outside an enormous, dilapidated castle. Above the door, engraved in stone, was a sign that read: "Thavian Darknoll 1402."

1402? That was nearly six hundred years—

Something pricked me in the arm. I turned in horror as Darknoll leaned over me, injecting me with a green liquid from a syringe. Before I could react, my limbs went numb, and I blacked out.

When I regained consciousness, I was on my back, staring at a stone ceiling. I blinked and tried to move my head, but was unable. I blinked again, trying to reclaim my senses and mobility. After a moment, I felt bindings on my legs and wrists and across my waist. My head was bound in a metal faceplate that covered my mouth and my neck.

I wished the faceplate had covered my nose. The castle smelled of mildew, musty rock, and highly fermented liquor—but I didn't believe it was liquor.

I tried to scream, but the faceplate muffled it.

"You're awake."

Something clicked, and the table I was bound to tilted up until I was upright, bringing me face-to-face with my captor.

Professor Darknoll wore a leather apron over his suit, rubber gloves, and goggles on his head. His hair was wild, and he had scratched his temple raw.

"Welcome to my laboratory, Allan," Darknoll said with a sweeping gesture. "I fear this is a bit premature. I hadn't intended to bring you here until I was certain I had learned all I could from you, but you left me no choice. You see, I can't afford for you to lose any money or any more respect with your father."

My brows furrowed.

He walked to a table laden with bottles, tubes, and chemicals. An automaton assisted him with pouring chemicals into beakers at precise measurements. He gave a few instructions to the automaton and then stepped in front of me again, examining me like an animal in a cage.

"You will be the youngest I've ever possessed, but all the better for me. You are healthy, and I have ensured you eat well."

My eyes widened. *Possessed?*

As if reading my thoughts, the professor laughed. "I told you the Good Book inspired me intellectually, had I not? Did I tell you how? Or what passage exactly? No? Recall our first conversation on *The Unnatural History of Death*. Man must conquer death. But not by spiritual means. Eternity shouldn't be earned in servitude."

He scratched his temple. "Think of the story of the possessed man in the graveyard. Supposedly, a *legion* of demons lived in him. Many stories depicted possessions, but that one stuck with me above all others. It gave me an idea. Not many in one man, but one man in many!" He clapped his hands together; the smack reverberated off the stone walls. "And so I have conquered death, Allan! For nearly six hundred years, I have defied God and nature!"

He moved to a wide, four-tiered shelf that held jars. Hundreds of jars. I had to blink several times before I recognized what the jars held.

Brains.

Sweat broke from every pore in my body. Tears ran from my eyes, my body desperate to shed the fear that surged within me.

"For years, I struggled to master how to preserve what is most important," Darknoll said, returning to the table. "My mind. My body may wilt, but my mind must live on. I sacrificed the townspeople to perfect my method. The right chemical to preserve the brain until it is transferred to another body, another to stimulate the body to accept the new organ. And the old is collected and studied for future purposes. As yours will be."

More tears fell, and I groaned.

"Not to worry, Allan. I will be a good son to your father and mother. You wanted to return wiser, and you shall.

"These chemicals are expensive, as is the maintenance on the automatons who help with my procedure. It costs money, and my own fortune won't survive another lifetime. Yours, however, will. And I may someday follow in my new father's footsteps and make way for more...acceptable means for me to practice my method."

Hearing the man speak of stealing my life, my family, was too much for me. But there was nothing I could do. I couldn't move. I was destined to be a jar on his shelf.

Another automaton entered, this one much larger. He had a round head but not the usual blue eyes. It approached and examined me with dark red eyes. The light fell on my face, bathing me in its eerie glow. One hand was anatomically correct, but the other was a saw blade.

"Can't have you moving." Darknoll snickered. "The exact measurement of your head must be discerned. The slightest cut in the wrong place could kill us both." He scratched his raw temple, drawing blood. "In a few minutes, I will be in the same position as you. But I will wake again with a new lifetime!"

The buzzsaw whirred and drew closer. I closed my eyes and tried to cry out one last time.

Darknoll's laughter ripped through the air. "*I* am legion! *I* am many!"

An explosion erupted. My eyes burst open. The buzzsaw automaton had a hole in its head. Wires and sparks sputtered out like mechanical gore. It shook for a few seconds before it fell over.

Darknoll shrieked and foamed as he ran to his table, grabbing a syringe. "Who dare—"

Another explosion and Darknoll's head jerked back.

He crashed into the table, glass shattered, and chemicals soaked him. His body slumped to the floor. Lifeless gray eyes gazed at me with a hole in his forehead.

I froze, not daring to believe my captor was dead.

A man appeared before me, slipping a pistol into a holster under his tan coat. He had mutton chops and a bowler hat.

The man outside the restaurant.

"You should have listened to your father, Allan," he said, freeing my head. "I tried to remind you."

I gasped. "Who are you?"

"Michael Pennington at your service. Detective and sometimes bodyguard. I work for your father. Sorry I didn't get here sooner."

"How...how did you know I was in trouble?" I asked as he worked on the bindings around my wrists.

"I didn't exactly. I couldn't find much on the professor prior to his time at the university. Your father only wanted me to follow and to be ready in case you were in any real danger. Nothing more. When you disappeared on an unlisted train, I knew something was wrong. I took a carriage along the track until I found the train."

My ankles were freed, and I stumbled into Detective Pennigton's arms, Darknoll's chemicals still in my veins.

"Thank you," I rasped.

"Ready to go home?" he inquired.

I tried to nod, but my head only rolled to the side. "Yes."

"That would be wise," Pennington said, supporting me.

Wise. It was my ignorant admiration of Darknoll that nearly made me another victim to his pursuit of immortality, but it was my father's wisdom that saved me. One day I would be independent and choose my friends with all the wisdom my father could instill.

As Pennington assisted me out of the laboratory, past broken automatons with bullet holes, and into the morning light, I was grateful that the only thing possessing me was the need to be at my father's side.

This Foe of Mine
by Crystal Grant

It watches me. Judges me. Mocks me and frightens me.
Follows me around wherever I go.
Behind me, beside me, even right under me.
Chained to my neck with my spirit in tow.

This trail of cold darkness leaks all around.
Blends with the shade. Grows in the dark.
Like a stain of black tar, spilled on the ground.
It never leaves. I never breathe. We're never apart.

This burden is starting to tire me, wear on me.
Pressing in, darkening, dampening my soul.
Pierces me. Weighs on me. Grasps at me. Breathes on me.
Stays with me always, laughing—my shadow.

Yes, I'm afraid of my own silhouette.
It's mocked and tormented for years.

It hovers above me like an overdue debt.
Beats at me, pounds on me, drives me to tears.

But I've found a sword to dispel that old foe.
A light, a weapon of strength, might, and power.
And wherever it aims, that darkness must go.
So though I may tremble, I no longer cower.

Now I'm a clumsy warrior and may drop it on my toe.
But I keep it ever close to me, never out of sight.
So when my shadow tries to lurk, mean and dark and cold,
I raise my sword, stare him down, drive him back into the
night!

Widow Rose

by Lara E. Madden

The widow twists the wedding ring off her finger. Throughout the mansion, lights flicker. She slips the ring onto a chain and hangs it around her neck. *I can't let it go just yet. Soon. But not tonight.*

She brushes rouge across her cheeks, refreshes her lipstick, sets her curls with hairspray, and tucks the ring beneath the collar of her dress. The widow's eyes burn as she stares intently into the mirror, looking beyond her reflection.

"This one's going to be different," she tells the glass. "I really like this man. And I need to be free to move on." She wipes a brisque hand under her eyes, refusing to cry and ruin her mascara. "I deserve to be happy," she says, but her voice is shaking. The wind blows outside, and the old house creaks and groans in protest.

The widow goes downstairs and begins to light the

table candles. She plays an old record that she and her husband used to dance to when he was alive. Five minutes before her date is meant to arrive, she puts dinner out so it will still be steaming hot when she uncovers the platters. She smiles at the set table. It will be a wonderful night in the company of a good man whom she likes very much. It is still infatuation, mind you. Not love. Not like what she'd once had with her Marvin. But there is certainly something there.

The ancient doorbell chimes through the house. She races to the door and embraces the man with the bouquet of bright crimson roses. When he steps across the threshold, he takes her hand, weaving his fingers between hers. Her chest tightens, and she smiles because she'd forgotten that the spaces between her fingers do not need to be empty forever.

She shows him to the table she set for them, pours the wine she has been saving for a very long time, and tells him not to worry when the floor begins to shake beneath them so hard the wine glasses tremble.

"Minor earthquakes are common here," she says, repeating some geology and physics phrases she's learned for explaining away the house's unusual phenomenon. She doesn't tell him that this is the second house she's lived in since Marvin's death or that the tremors follow her wherever she goes.

The supper—a lovely roast with vegetables that was her husband's favorite meal—is nearly flawless, but the lights keep flickering on and off throughout the course of the dinner and the candles blow out at random. Every time, the widow rolls her eyes in the dark and relights them while muttering under her breath. Her date laughs and makes a joke of the odd repetitive coincidences, saying something about the house's draftiness and a good contractor he knows.

They talk for hours, the words coming naturally, the silences between the words so comfortable and easy. She does not need to *try* to enjoy his company. The loneliness of the house is dissipating, like winter cold in a room where a fire has just been lit. The widow had forgotten how good *togetherness* feels. It has been many, many years since the last time she fell in love.

She starts a slow jazz record that makes the man smile. He stands, reaches out a hand, and asks her to dance. She doesn't know if she remembers how, but when his hand finds the curve of her waist, and they fall into step with the music, it is as if they have always danced together, as if they have known each other for many long years. When the man leans in closer, and she lifts her head to kiss him, everything feels right. Their time together is like a story that has already been written: inevitable, obvious, perfect. *Maybe this is how the rest of my life begins,* the widow lets herself believe as the man's kisses find her jaw, her neck, her shoulder.

She hears the wind beating the house harder, the creaks and shaking walls growing louder, and out of the corner of her eye, the chandelier swings slightly. She sighs and tells her guest that she needs a moment to freshen up. She leaves him alone in the living room and passes through the kitchen to speak with her late husband privately.

Beside the refrigerator, the vase of roses lays in fragments on the marble tile. The record scratches violently from the dining room, and all the candles blow out as she walks past to the bathroom.

The widow checks her lipstick in the mirror, and the glass fogs up without any steam in the room.

"You have to understand," she whispers harshly to the mirror. "You have to let me go this time. You aren't alive anymore. I need to be allowed to love again."

From the other side of the mirror, letters appear.

*MY*ROSE

Marvin's old nickname for her.

"No!" the widow says. "You will not ruin this for me! I said, '*till death* do us part,' my love, and it has been much longer than that now. You need to stop this! Stop haunting me and *be a proper dead person*!" She is taking the tone she always takes when they have fights, the one Marvin hated when he was alive. The lights flicker again. She hears a picture frame fall and break in the hallway and knows it's their wedding photo. The mirror rattles harder and harder until a small crack forms at one corner, reaching down across the foggy letters.

Rose turns her back on the splintering glass and ignores the ghost. She stands a little taller and brushes a wrinkle out of her dress, shuts the bathroom door definitively, goes back through the dark kitchen, and sways into the living room, where her guest is—

Time stops. Rose is losing herself in her screaming, in the pool of blood on the floor, her date lying face-down in it, dead.

She struggles to turn him over, pounding on his chest to wake him up, sobbing into his shirt, smearing blood on her face in the process.

Blood everywhere. Blood from his throat, from the long gash across it, cut with a thick piece of glass that is embedded deep in his neck, broken off of a shattered window. *All* of the windows have shattered.

Marvin has never killed anyone before, never done more than scare men away.

Rose tries frantically to find a pulse, to see the man's

chest rise. Her own heart pounds in her ears, and her breathing is so fast she feels dizzy, as if her body is trying to make up for the dead man's horrible stillness. Her hands close in tight fists, bunching the cloth of his shirt, trying desperately to make sense of what she sees.

Behind her, there's the slight sound of a chandelier shuddering, and she snaps her head around to glare at it. The bulbs burn out, and the chandelier goes dark. In another room, there's creaking, like a man nervously shifting his weight. Ashamed of himself.

This is too much. He's crossed every line now. He's become something wicked. A monster.

Slowly, Rose opens her fists and looks at them. The man's blood covers her hands. It stains her dress and drips down her arms. She stares at her hands held out in front of her until her shock starts to freeze over and turn to cold, sharp fury.

Rose slips in the blood as she struggles to her feet, sobbing, wailing, groaning, screaming. Her body is shaking, and her voice tearing with rage and grief, both emotions building on each other and coming in waves that boil up and over as she surges through the house like a storm.

She tracks blood as she runs down the halls, screams at the walls, slams on the tables, shatters plates and glasses, smashes records, and throws things at mirrors.

"MARVIN!!!" Her shouts quake through the mansion with more ferocity than she realized she is capable of, her voice wavering in an animal wail. With this final sorrowful, vengeful crescendo, she collapses on the floor and sobs until all the energy in her body is exhausted.

She cannot move the corpse tonight. She will have to bury him in the morning.

This one was supposed to be different...

She can't think of it now, cannot even look at the face of the dead man in the living room. Cannot wonder what could have been or what will happen tomorrow. Cannot even weep for him anymore tonight.

"I just don't understand how you could do this, Marvin," she whispers. Her heart is on the floor, broken like the man whose blood is crusting in the carpet. "I thought you loved me."

Another tear slips off the bridge of her nose as she crawls back up the stairs. She is too tired and too alone to stand. To walk. So she pulls herself up the steps on her hands and knees.

"This isn't *love*, Marvin." Her words are so soft that she wonders if he can hear her at all. "You're killing me. The loneliness is dragging the life out of me. I can't keep on surviving this way."

He always hears her. He listens better now than he did

when he was alive, but he's still just as stubborn, just as jealous.

In her fog, Rose finds her way back to the bedroom. When she feels the wedding ring hanging around her neck, she yanks the necklace free and tosses it away halfheartedly—her unofficial divorce from the dead man. Weary to the bone, she pulls the large comforter around her and falls asleep, whispering over and over, "Marvin, you have to let me go. You have to. Please. Let me go. If you love me, Marvin..."

Letters appear on the last unbroken mirrors in the house. The widow sees them in the morning when she is cleaning up the broken glass and ordering new carpet.

There's a single flower waiting for her on the kitchen table, the only one that hasn't been trampled or torn. She throws it down and crushes it under her heel.

As she walks away from it, she makes up her mind that she will never respond to the name 'Rose' again.

Widow Rose

I'M SORRY, EVELYN

reads a mirror in the bathroom.

I WENT TOO FAR THIS TIME

says the one in the spare bedroom.

In the living room above the fireplace,

YOU'RE FREE NOW.

The Lady of the Moors
by L.A. Thornhill

Long ago in a kingdom ancient and forlorn
Dwelt the Baron Euric of a dying line.
A wealthy man filled with anger and much scorn.
To find a maiden to wed, he did resign.
Thus in a village, he found the fair Madeline.
A maid of strength, virtue, humble piety.
But Euric only saw her beauty—so divine!
Kidnapped to his castle, caused her anxiety,
Demanded she bond to his society.

Madeline, with a strong heart of resolve,
Denied Euric his demand for wedded vows.
But the wicked man made her will dissolve.
He threatened to steal the farm her family plows,
And leave them with nothing to ever endow.
Madeline, knowing her family to be poor,
Consented to the foul union before a crowd

Of the Baron's friends, while a chaplain did mourn
Madeline's fate—now the Lady of the Moors.

That night Euric and his friends enjoyed a feast.
They drank strong spirits, laughed without remorse.
Madeline, through the halls in the castle's east,
Escaped the revelers and he who did force
Madeline to alter her life's chosen course.
She quietly crept across the castle floor,
Her steps silenced as men spoke in drunken discourse.
Finally, she reached the castle's golden door,
And found herself in the embrace of the moors.

"The thoughts you think, they are utterly unwise.
Do you not know why these dark moors bring dread?"
The voice startled Madeline more than advised.
She saw a hag with a flame, hair dingy red.
"You venture forth," said the hag. "Soon you'll be dead."
Madeline replied, "I'll give him nothing more.
I would rather die than share his wicked bed."
The hag laughed. "Euric is nothing to adore.
But think twice before stepping on the moor."

The hag then wove a dark and foreboding tale
Of the moor outside Euric's castle, vast and far.

Cruel and evil men, and souls who were frail,
Vanished among rocks and bogs, thick like tar.
At night their souls awoke when dim be the stars.
The spirits sought others to share their fate.
Victims of Euric's ancestors, who now are
Forever wandering with nothing to abate
Their fear of the light and their dreadful state.

Madeline, fearful of her new husband,
Did seize the hag's lantern and faced,
Against all warning, the haunted moorland.
Better to challenge spirits than be disgraced
By the Baron, who would undoubtedly give chase
To Madeline once he realized she'd gone.
She dashed into the moor, not leaving a trace
For Euric to find lest her efforts be withdrawn;
She prayed to be out of the moors by dawn.

For several yards, Madeline did flee with fright
Past sharp rocks and branches and unseen drops.
A starless night. A lantern, her only light.
After many minutes she came to a stop.
She lifted her light and peered from a hilltop.
The wedding party ran along the castle grounds.
They mounted horses, all ready to gallop.

At seeing pursuers, Madeline's heart did pound;
She ran back to the moors, where mist did shroud.

Deeper she traversed. Madeline panted and gasped
In the darkness as rocks and twigs tore her bare feet.
From the depths of the mist came a voice that rasped:
"You should not have left the castle keep!
And now you will join us in the bogs deep!"
Madeline shrieked, raised her lantern, and searched
The mist around, but saw nothing creep.
She groaned. Her heart ached. Her stomach lurched.
No other sound. Not even an owl from where it perched.

One sound broke the silence—an icy crack!
She gazed at her lantern and gave a fright.
The glass was broken from an unseen attack!
A nervous inspection found only dim light.
Still the maiden pressed on, deeper into the night.
She clung to her protector, determined to endure.
"Your efforts are futile! We'll put out your light!"
Whether she would survive, Madeline was unsure.
But on she walked, this Lady of the Moors.

The wind picked up and the mist unfurled
Revealing the wicked spirits about her—foul and fell!

Floating shallow faces, cobweb-like hair that swirled.
Madeline wept, her candlelight did ebb and swell
As she looked upon the torments of hell.
From within the mist hands reached out and gave
Madeline cause to panic and run 'til she fell
Down a hill and stumbled into a shallow grave.
Soon to be a victim of these cursed knaves!

Madeline clawed for her light, her fate sealed.
But she saw her hope broken in the grass.
The candle's wick held a small flame for her to feel
The dying heat as she readied for her life to pass.
She focused on the embers and broken glass
And not on the spirits who drew near with doom.
The flame sank into the earth, under lantern of brass.
Then came an idea that vanquished her gloom.
Hope in Madeline's soul—like a flower—did bloom!

Madeline ripped up grass by the handfuls
Carefully laying them over the last of her fire.
The flame grew in size, causing all the dreadful
Spirits about her to cry for depths of the mire.
Madeline laughed with delight. No longer dire!
She snatched up twigs and leaves, and giddily
Built against the darkness a makeshift pyre.

L.A. Thornhill

With a stronger flame she set ablaze a nearby tree
And, all night, celebrated her victory.

On several empty-saddled horses came
News of Baron Euric who fell off his steed
And was taken by the spirits. For they did blame
Him for the fate from which they'd never be freed.
With the Baron dead it was quickly decreed
That Madeline inherit. And for ages she'd ensure
That the spirits—on the lost—would no longer feed.
Her descendants built lit paths for the rich and the poor.
So to honor with light, the Lady of the Moors.

The Forest

by Megan Mullis

I stood at the edge of the path,
eyes flickering between the thick weft of trees,
and my family that had ventured on ahead,
I hadn't been forgotten,
but I felt alone,
kicking at stones,
I did not know how lost I was then.

The forest beckoned me,
'come forth,'
that sickeningly sweet chorus of voices,
singing from the deep,
melodies of hatred hidden,
behind a veil of love made cheap,
a beautiful mask decorated in dark stones,
all of them false promises of held worth.

I decided it better to go,
to find my family,
but intrigued as I was naive,
I stayed to watch the show.

The forest welcomed me,
like I was only a visitor,
like it only expected me to be a visitor,
but knew more,
I followed a black butterfly into the night,
there were no stars,
and though hard to see,
she was clearer than anything else,
mesmerized,
I did not see the vines pooling at my boots,
twining like serpents around my ankles.

I found myself lost in the forest,
the static of leaves crackling in my ears,
I stood still,
and listened to the branches creak,
the ground quake,
the flowers shake,
as the beast grew near to me.

The Forest

He came to me as a dark shadow,
a wisp of smoke under a starless sky,
he whispered in my ear,
every doubt and stress and fear,
his voice so near and dear,
like that of an old friend,
like I'd know him long ago,
or he'd known me maybe,
maybe he knew my father,
voice passed down for centuries,
genetically from family to family,
like an inheritance,
or a curse.

I stepped back,
but as his sentences morphed back into static,
it followed me into the deep,
I caught the butterfly in the corner of my eye,
but she became a snake,
then a bear,
then a meek little church mouse,
and she skittered away into the underbrush.

I made a house in the forest,
a rickety shelter of vines and string,

there were no lights,

but I wasn't scared of the dark any longer,

fears were a past memory,

I knew where my monster was,

I knew what he sounded like,

I was not troubled to run from him,

or maybe I couldn't.

I convinced myself my home was in the forest,

that I needed nothing more,

that I wasn't cold,

or numb,

or hungry,

I wasn't alone,

I had my monster,

and my butterfly/snake/bird/mouse,

sometimes I saw her again

she slithered or skittered or growled,

I had the leaves of the trees and the sound of static,

I needed nothing but the blood that dripped,

from the vines like syrup,

or an open wound,

and rain poured down on wildflowers,

that never lived long enough to bloom,

I planted seeds that never grew,

The Forest

and shooed away any particles of light,
that showed through a thick canopy,
all while having no idea what to do,
I didn't breathe once,
but I didn't need to.

When the nights were drawn on,
old and sleepless,
when screams could be heard through the trees,
children lost in a sea of lonely,
somewhere out there but too far to meet gaze with,
too long gone,
but just out of reach,
when screams ripped from my throat like weeds from a
dead garden,
I was unheard,
it was lost in the static and the birds' strangled chirps,
because the forest hears no one,
don't you know that,
you naive child,
you should have left when you could,
I should have gone back,
I should have tried harder to be happy when I had the
chance,
so I quieted my voice,

because clearly, I was not trapped,
I should not cry wolf,
when I came here by choice.

He came to me as a diagnosis,
but I knew then he was more than a pill could push back,
I screamed at him,
and he echoed,
I ran and he followed,
I burned the house to the ground,
and he wrapped me up like a blanket constrictor,
snarled like a bear,
told me he'd be my home,
told me I was nothing,
told me I was dust,
told me I owned nothing,
and I owed everything.

The smile he gave when I listened,
was more terrifying than death itself,
so I cut him open like a surgeon,
and ran with the vines still around my ankles.

I found my family at the edge of the forest,
the light bright enough to blind,

The Forest

the forest screamed for me,
but I did not hear it,
the monster stared,
but I did not see him.

I caught the butterfly in the corner of my eye,
trapped like a prisoner in a house of shadow and static,
she knew how to be everything but her own,
she knew how to hide it better than I did,
she'd been there longer than I was,
I call for her sometimes,
and I wonder if she hears me,
I hope one day she finds her way out.

I keep the forest in a lock box,
I threw away the key,
but it still finds a way to find me sometimes,
now and then,
but again,
I remind myself,
that my monster is only a church mouse,
if I do not let him be anything else.

The Forbidden Library
by Anne J. Hill

R umors of ghosts and hauntings shrouded the library thicker than the morning fog. An October chill warded off all but the most resolute souls. And yet, a nervous woman in a rustling brown dress stood before the door, gripping an opened letter in her right hand.

A shiver crept from her hand to her neck and then down her spine. She'd spent the whole morning pouring over the letter's words and rattling them around in her brain. This library *had* to hold answers.

A black cat laid curled up by the doorway with his chin buried between his paws. His green eyes blinked lazily up at her with a heavy flick of his tail, examining the newcomer.

The "B" in the building's title had long ago cracked and fallen onto the porch, leaving behind "LI RARY." The lady tiptoed past the "B" rubble and reached for the door handle. Her fingers touched the cold metal, and she paused, the note's pleading words still running through her head:

Meet me at the library at sunset. Bring no one. The rumors are true. -The Librarian

The rumors... Of course, she knew ghosts weren't real, so she wasn't worried about that. But there hadn't been a librarian in years, and *someone* had sent the letter to her, a burnt-out writer who preferred escaping her own failure by going on adventures written by other authors.

Steadying her breathing, she twisted the handle, a resounding creak echoing throughout the whole library, and stepped inside. Immediately, the door slammed shut, and the room engulfed her in heavy darkness. She gasped, moldy decay filling her lungs, and the letter slipped from her fingers to the floor.

"Grace..." a feathery male voice drifted from nowhere.

Her heart thudded in her ears, drowning out the silence that followed with a *lub dub, lub dub, lub dub.*

She blinked several times before faint shapes started sharpening at the edges of the rotting room. A soft light twinkled in the darkness from the top of a winding staircase. She swallowed thick air and crept toward it. The floorboards moaned as if being woken from a deep slumber.

Reaching the first step, she tilted her head back to look up at the light. A cloaked silhouette drifted over it.

"H—hello?" she croaked.

The light vanished. Sweat crawled down her back, chilled by the cold air. A gust of wind shoved her stumbling back onto the floor. A flame sparked in her face, blinding her momentarily. The candlelight lowered, revealing a smiling face with glowing red eyes.

"Hello, Grace." The phantom's female voice contrasted the previous one, and its stale, icy breath wafted over her.

She wanted to turn and run, but her body forgot how to move, stricken with fear and cemented to the floorboards.

She dared not speak.

The pale face cocked to the side and looked her over. "Welcome to the Forbidden Library, where dreams come to die, and stories turn to dust."

Grace trembled, taking in the creature fully—a floating cloak with the blurred image of a woman underneath, begging to be made solid. A flickering lantern dangled from her translucent hand.

"Afraid to speak?" the ghost asked, almost teasingly. "I imagined as much. You've been lacking in words as of late." Her eyes danced like the flame in the lantern.

Grace forced down the bile that was rising in her throat and took a step backward, but the ghost was soon inches from her face again. She took a chance and squeaked, "Who

271

are you? The Librarian?"

The ghost's head tilted back, and she let out a burst of amused laughter. "Who am I, you ask? Why, don't you know?" She floated around Grace, circling as if inspecting her for purchase. "But then again, you never did have the decency to name me." She swung the lantern, grinning. "The others call me Torch."

Grace blinked, then blinked again. "Torch? You're... Why should *I* name you?"

Torch rolled her fiery eyes. "You'll figure it out. Follow the light, Grace. The light..." Torch and her lantern dissipated, and all was still. "...will lead the way..."

The whistling wind from outside was the only sound until, somewhere, a bow touched down on strings, and the mournful drawl of a cello echoed through the library.

Lantern light appeared at the top of the spiral staircase again, and this time, Grace followed it, fingers running timidly along the cold, dusty railing.

At the top, Torch waited. Behind her was a long, narrow hallway. Torch floated several yards ahead of Grace as she led, the weeping cello following them to the middle of the hall.

In one heartbeat, the cello's tune, Torch, and the light burst into nothingness.

"Stop leaving!" Grace swung her fist toward the wall,

but she didn't make contact with the rotting wood. She stumbled, newfound panic setting in. She felt like cotton balls were being shoved down her throat, a hand was tightening around her neck, and a stack of books was pressing down on her chest. She clawed at the oppressive air, searching for something, anything.

"Grace..." the male voice from earlier whispered, piercing deep into her wavering confidence.

The floor seemed to fall away beneath her feet. The darkness overtook her, and she screamed, "Let me out! I want out! In the name of all things good, let me out!"

Her voice disappeared into the void, and the only response she got was her own labored breathing.

Then, when Grace had almost given up hope, the haunted strings resumed their nocturn, and dozens of candles burst into light, lining the edges of the hallway, all the way to the foot of a cello. The bow moved across the strings with no hands to control it, and Grace's legs nearly failed her.

"What *is* good, Miss Grace?" a low voice spoke from behind her, different still from the two earlier voices.

Grace jumped and turned to see a bony man—pale to the point of translucency—whose dark hair swayed in an ethereal wind across his shoulders. His mouth was straight with a touch of sorrow, his eyes sunken in pain.

"W—what?" Grace stammered. He felt so...familiar.

"In the name of all things good... What *is* good? Is there *anything* good in your world? I see flames, and knives, and nooses, and abandonment, and wars, and death, and betrayal. Is there *any* good?" His voice lived in a land between singing and speaking.

Grace studied him like his face might hold all the answers to her most profound questions. She felt a heart-wrenching need to help him. "I don't know... What world are you talking about? What's your name?"

Tears trickled down his face, and he muttered, "Lark. You must save us..." The man, apparently Lark, grabbed her wrist in desperation before vanishing with a petrifying shriek.

Grace stumbled back, thrown into darkness as the cello and candles died away.

Grief overwhelmed her. She did not know why, but she burst into tears. Her heart slammed against her chest, sending waves of pain and sorrow through her body. It was like the weight of the world was living inside of her.

No, not *this* world. Another world. And yet, a world she was deeply connected to.

In the darkness, she finally understood.

Torch, who needed a name, and Lark, who needed freedom.

These were her characters from a book she'd abandoned years ago when her husband had left her. Heart-pounding terror set in. She shivered at the thought of who else might be alive in this library.

"Okay, I get it!" she yelled to the black void. "You're my characters! Will you release me now?"

She was met with a blazing fire that shot out and scorched the ceiling, illuminating the whole hallway.

And a dragon, breathing hot fumes in her face.

"B—Blastrin?" She shuddered.

He flapped his wings and shoved his head against her, pushing her backward until she staggered through an open doorway, Blastrin's flames a beacon in the dark.

"Grace..." the hidden voice tickled her ear as she straightened herself. She glanced around, hoping to find the source at last. Instead, she found the new room was lined with rows of shelves. Shelves that should have held books, but instead of stories, they were being overtaken by vines.

And the plant life was slowly tearing the bookshelves apart.

She knew which of her characters must be responsible for this abomination. "Ivy?" she called, standing braver than before. Something about knowing made the darkness less intimidating.

Until a vine looped around her ankles and threw her up

in the air, dangling her upside down.

"Ivy, put me down!"

A green-haired girl sat cross-legged on a table. "I will. If you promise me something."

"Anything!"

Ivy gave a lopsided grin. "Set us free." The words rolled off her tongue, a mischievous twinkle in her eye.

Grace trembled in her binds. "How? I promise!"

The vine dropped her, and she plummeted into the rotted floor, the force of her body shattering through the wood. She covered her face as she crashed through what felt like endless rooms until she made contact with a cement ground.

She groaned. A supernatural force must have protected her from shattering every bone, but it had done nothing for the pain.

"That's one way to make an entrance," someone said.

Grace pushed herself up, rubbed dust and debris from her eyes, and took in her surroundings.

Stone walls, flickering sconces, and...books! Hundreds of books on shelves lined the walls—some closed, and others opened to blank pages, not a word in sight.

"Welcome to my Book Dungeon!" the feminine voice spoke again.

Grace squinted, the dust settling around her.

Teetering atop a bookshelf was a woman about Grace's age. Her legs swung, and she grinned a lifeless smile. "Hiya! Please tell me you know who I am? Need a hint?" She didn't wait for a reply before singing off key about a girl named Polly and her dolly.

"Polly." Grace nodded, though she'd known the moment she saw her unmistakable white hair and flower crown.

"Righto!" She jumped off the bookshelf.

"How do I get out of here?"

Polly tilted her head, burrowing her eyes into Grace's soul. "Write!" She stretched out her hand, and an array of candles lit up a dilapidated desk with a rusted typewriter on top.

Polly pulled a book from the shelf and flipped open to the title page. It read: *Friendly Knives* by Grace Hunter. She set the book down in Grace's arms.

"Finish it. Finish it and set us free."

Grace thumbed the pages. "I can't." Her throat tightened, anxiety from years past resurfacing.

Polly's face dropped, staring at the floor in sorrow. "I want to be *seen*. I want to be *heard*. Let me be seen, Grace."

And then Polly was gone.

Grace stood, holding the pages of her unfinished story, her body aching from the fall and her skin crawling in the cold. She groaned and kicked at a rotten piece of wood. "Stop doing that! Stop leaving me!"

"Grace..." the voice returned, but this time it had a face. Stepping out of the shadows was a glowing man who much resembled Lark, only his body was almost solid, and he smiled through deep-set pain.

She knew who he was.

"The Librarian," she said with bated breath.

The Librarian, Lark's twin, reached his hand out to her. "Come, Grace. Write."

Grace shook her head, hugging the closed book to her chest. "I can't. You know I can't."

He patiently smiled and nodded with greater understanding than any living person could have. "I do, because I'm a part of you. But, Grace, you forgot to finish me." He lifted his hand, and it flickered between solid and translucent. "I need to be more than a half-formed thought."

Grace pushed back tears. "I can't go back there! You know that!" Her fingers tightened around the book, wanting to tear the words apart.

The Librarian lowered himself to the floor, crossing his blinking legs. His sympathetic smile remained, and she knew he felt everything inside of her as he quietly waited.

Grace slammed the book to the floor. "Why did I have

to write you this way! Stop knowing things and always being right." She buried her face into her hands, breathing through the gaps in her fingers. "Fine." She glanced over at The Librarian.

He nodded. "Remember, Grace, don't abandon your gifts in the midst of pain. Sometimes, they are the light you need. Write." He nodded toward the desk.

Grace swallowed down the lies her husband had installed in her, how she would amount to nothing and be forever alone.

She retrieved the book, set it down beside the typewriter, and began typing. With each keystroke, the words appeared on the blank pages of the book.

The words weren't special. They weren't crafty and well-edited. They were just words to be cleaned up later. But they embodied the life of her characters. And all that mattered right then was setting them free. Completing their stories. Not leaving them in the darkness she had thrown them into because of her own unresolved pain.

So, she typed away to the tune of the cello, the flickering of the candlelight, and the supportive presence of The Librarian. Something brushed against her leg. She looked down and saw the black cat from the porch cozying up to her. She smiled, surprised she hadn't thought of it before. "Hello, Brin."

The Librarian's cat blinked green, piercing eyes at her with a longing meow.

Grace offered him a smile, the terror from before melting away with each keystroke. The lives of her creations were finding their endings.

She'd forgotten how much she loved this book. A renewed fervor rushed through her, and as the first rays of morning peaked through a high window carved into the stone, she typed the two greatest words: The end.

The Librarian, satisfied, drifted from the floor and into her book.

Grace leaned back in her chair, a pleased smile warming her face.

It was only then that she noticed the cello had stopped, Brin had gone, and the lights had returned. Picking up her finished first draft, she stood.

All the decay and rubble had left, replaced with bright candles, finished books, and Torch's lantern sitting alone in the middle of the floor.

Her characters had been set free, and now, she realized, so had she.

When Darkness Breathes His Last
by Savannah Jezowski

The Darkness stretches out his hand,
Confident of his reach,
Joyous in the terror he spreads
As long his shadow grows.
For the night is his, always his,
Until at last it's not—
That moment right before the dawn
Is what the Darkness fears.

The Darkness crafts the nightmare
That holds men in its grip,
The chilling thoughts that suck poor souls
Of all that gives them life.
For the dream is his, always his,
Until at last it's not—
For the dream also gives men hope
When Darkness breathes its last.

The Darkness owns the battlefield
Where brave men give it all,
The graveyard where the brave and true
Become the worn and lost.
For the war is his, always his,
Until at last it's not—
For that last stand of untold valor
Is what the Darkness fears.

The Darkness revels in the sorrow
That haunts each waking thought,
How he delights to see the loss
Inflicted by his reign.
For such loss is his, always his,
Until the joke's on him—
For pain is what gives good men strength
To fight another day,

To fight and slay the dragons
That haunt their every step,
To climb out of the deep abyss
With courage left intact.
When all is lost, then all is gained,
And swords slip free of stone.
When morning breaks beyond the pit
Then Darkness breathes his last.

"The light shines in the darkness,
and the darkness has not overcome it."
-John 1:5 (NIV)

Acknowledgments

It takes a village to raise a book.

This book would not be what it is today without the help of so many different people.

I'd first like to thank Lara E. Madden, my best friend, housemate/tenant, fellow word bender, fire dancing wanderer, and anthology right-hand man. Without hours spent pouring over submissions, brainstorming, editing, and endless laughter that caused coffee to come out of my nose, this book, and all of my future books, wouldn't exist. Here's to many more years of fake sword fights and telling you not to set my house on fire. Thank you!

Here's to my mom and dad for their endless support of me in general, and especially to Mom for my writing. The best support is the kind that gives advice on how to improve and encourages you to keep moving forward, and that's been both of you. Specifically for this book, a conversation with my mom about why I write "dark" stories and miscommunication of what that actually means helped narrow in on the theme. Following that conversation, and after a long talk with God about it, I concluded that this book needed to purposefully use the darkness to amplify the light and not just be dark for darkness' sake. So, thank you, Mom, for that nudge in the right direction and for your help in editing several of the stories within these pages.

Thank you to my brother, Erin Nathaniel, for a lifetime of book and story discussions late into the night. Thank you for being my sounding board on the graphic design side of things and editing the book cover.

I'd like to thank the rest of my immediate and extended family for sticking with me through the years, listening to my crazy ideas, giving sage advice, answering business questions, keeping my lights on (quite literally), discussing daily writing routines, sharing my excitement, critiquing my grammar, encouraging my creative mind, making up very odd ideas with me, teasing me, pointing me to God, and loving me unconditionally. Without you, I wouldn't be where I am now.

Thank you to all the teachers I've had through the years, but I'd like to highlight three in particular: Mrs. Frick, Mr. Schwartz, and Mrs. Hurley. Mrs. Frick expanded my love of good Literature and the importance of a theme being a complete sentence. Mr. Schwartz for pacing around the classroom reading *The Tell-Tale Heart* and making me fall in love with Poe and Dickens. Mrs. Hurley for installing the fundamental grammar that I now use daily in my editing and writing.

There are so many people to thank, and I could write a whole separate book about it, so for the sake of my readers, I'll keep this brief.

Thank you, Megan Mullis, for being our Poem Queen and ruling strictly over what poems are deemed worthy of this book. Thank you to Andrew Winch for stepping in to edit my short stories and several of Lara's. Thank you to Psycat Digital Ink & Motion for this stunning book cover. Thank you to Nathaniel Luscombe for making the publisher logo. Thank you to AJ Skelly, Beka Gremikova, Katie Marie, Effie Joe Stock, Teddi Deppner, and Kalie Night for my endless questions about publishing, marketing, contracts, and all that jazz. Thank you to Effie and Sarah Sutton for book formatting and dealing with my crazy deadlines. Thank you to Natalie Noel Truitt for brainstorming stories for this anthology and in general. Thank you to my writing support group (you girls rock!) and my anthology promotional team (who also rock!). Thank you to Effie, Ariel Choate, and Sarah Elliot for your artwork. Thank you to Katie, Crystal Grant, Savannah Jezowski, Laurel Jean, and Emily Barnett for jumping in to help edit last minute.

Thank you to my other housemate, Erin, for putting up with being told to feel book covers and being shamed for not liking the texture, and her toddler son, Psalm, for clapping over the same tiny things I do, like closing doors—literally. Thank you to all of Realm Makers Consortium for answering all my technical questions about self-publishing. Thank you to Frank Peretti for speaking at the Realm Maker's conference, inspiring me, and paving the way for speculative Christian Fiction. Thank you to Neil Gaiman for giving me a love for the dark fantasy genre and odd characters. And thank you to all the people who helped in one way or another who I might have missed in this long list. You're all very much appreciated!

Lastly, but most importantly, I'd like to thank God. I haven't always listened to Your voice, and You've still been faithful. Without Your guidance, discipline, love, and grace, I would be in a very different place, and this book would not exist.

-Anne J. Hill

About the Authors

Light Dawns in Darkness

Where Light Shines

There's Too Much to Say

It's Alive!

Forbidden Library

Anne J. Hill

Anne J. Hill is an author who enjoys writing fantasy for all ages. Her love of words has also led to her career as a freelance writer and editor. She spends her days dreaming up fantastical realms, talking out loud to the characters in her head, and rearranging her personal library, which has been affectionately dubbed the "Book Dungeon."

Where to find Anne:
www.annejhill.com
@anne.j.hill.editing

People Watchers

Don't Feed the Leprechauns

Widow Rose

Lara E. Madden

She might be crazy—the jury's still out—but Lara E. Madden would consider herself to be widely fascinated, with an affinity for wonder. She is madly in love with Jesus, with storytelling, and with the tribe of colorful characters that is her family and friends. When her feet are on the ground, she lives in Lancaster, PA with her three wonderful roommates, including Anne J. Hill, without whom she would likely never finish any project she starts. She is a novelist at heart but is currently focused on creating short fiction as she hones her writing craft. The stories included in this book are Lara's first published works.

You can find her on Instagram (@lara.e.madden),
Facebook (Lara Madden),
or at her blog, LaraTheWanderer.blogspot.com, which she
updates only very sparingly.

Immortals Anonymous
The Forest

Megan Mullis

Megan Mullis is a 17-year-old crazy cat lady, and an aspiring author with a poet's heart. Her poetry portrays her truth-seeking attitude. Some of her favorite poets include Edgar Allen Poe and Emily Dickinson, while drawing inspiration from Olivia Gatwood. She has a passion for writing about mental health, and she also loves photography, good books, deep conversations, and soft blankets.

Nightfall

D.A. Randall

D.A. Randall,
ThrillerWriter, was raised on
a steady diet of Batman,
James Bond, Star Trek and
Indiana Jones. He writes
fantasy and action
thrillers that read like
blockbuster movies.

You can find links to
all of his books and
events, and subscribe
to his Packing Action
newsletter at:

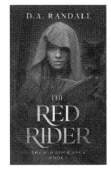
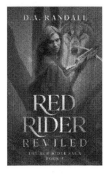

www.RandallAllenDunn.com.
You can also follow him on Facebook at:
https://www.facebook.com/RandallAllenDunn
Join the fan group, THE RED RIDERS of Wild
Street / La Rue Sauvage:
https://www.facebook.com/groups/945983672233767

A Taste of Life

Beka Gremikova

Beka Gremikova writes
folkloric fantasy from her
home in the Ottawa Valley,
Ontario Canada. When she's
not travelling, dabbling in
various art forms, or watching
anime, KDramas, and The
Great British Baking Show,
she can be found curled up in
the corner with a mystery
novel.

Links:

Website: www.bekagremikova.com
Instagram: www.instagram.com/beka.gremikova
Twitter: www.twitter.com/DreamofWriting
Facebook: www.facebook.com/bekagremikova
Author headshot credit: Sarah-Ann Wijngaarden.

The Guardian of the Maelstrom

Maseeha Seedat

Maseeha Seedat was born and raised in Johannesburg before moving to the Middle East at the age of seven. Her main novel, When Lightning Strikes, is still in the works, and it's an epic fantasy that follows the quest of twin sisters Heela and Flo as they try to save their parents from the tyrant king of Aellarion. The Guardian of the Maelstrom is her debut in the publishing world. As a young hijabi, she loves diversity and representation, and would choose found family over a romance any day. When she's not writing, Maseeha can be found chasing after her toddler cousin, jamming out to The Script, or clawing her way toward a degree in physiotherapy.

Website: sincerelymaseeha.weebly.com
IG: @sincerelymaseeha.writer
Twitter: @maseeha_writer

This Foe of Mine

Crystal Grant

Crystal Grant is a
book-collecting,
story-writing,
animal-loving,
wardrobe-seeking,
sword-wielding

(well, maybe not quite) daughter of God. She loves to read
and write stories with deep emotions and raw characters
who grow into warriors of faith.

Contact info:
Instagram: @crystalgrantfaithandfiction
Facebook: https://www.facebook.com/crystalgrantauthor
Website: www.crystalgrantfaithandfiction.com

The Headless Henwoman
and the Kissing Curse
Humble Pie

Kristiana Sfirlea

Kristiana Sfirlea is the author of the award-winning middle grade fantasy novel *Legend of the Storm Sneezer,* which won gold in the international Readers' Favorite Book Awards, as well as its sequel, *Legend of the Rainbow Eater.* She's a former haunted house operator, inspiring her delight in spooking readers, and she loves Jesus, her family, and imaginary life with her characters.

Where to buy her books: Amazon, Barnes & Noble, Indiebound, Bookshop.org, and almost anywhere books are sold!

Social media links:
Instagram: @KristianasQuill//Twitter: @KristianasQuill
Facebook: @KristianasQuillBooks
Website: www.KristianasQuill.com

Literary Lies

Kat Heckenbach

Kat Heckenbach graduated
from the University of
Tampa with a bachelor's
degree in biology, went on to
teach math, and then
homeschooled her son and
daughter while writing and
making sci-fi/fantasy art. She
is the author of YA
fantasy series Toch
Island Chronicles
and urban fantasy
Relent, as well as
dozens of fantasy,
science fiction, and
horror short stories
in magazines and anthologies.

Facebook:
https://www.facebook.com/KatHeckenbachAuthorArtist
Instagram: https://www.instagram.com/katheckenbach/
Twitter: https://twitter.com/KatHeckenbach
Website: http://katheckenbach.com/
Etsy shop: https://www.etsy.com/shop/JumpingRails/

Existence

Hollow

Still Waters

Denica McCall

Denica McCall is a young adult fantasy writer, poet, dreamer, and deep thinker who grew up in the Pacific Northwest and now resides in Kansas City where she enjoys working as a nanny, attending dance classes, drinking coffee, and planning her next travel adventure. She is currently working on her third YA novel which features fairies, a pegasus, and cave-stars.

Find out more and sign up for her newsletter to receive a free short story at http://denicamccall.com/.
Connect on Instagram: @denicamcauthor

Possession
Lady of the Moors

L.A. Thornhill

L.A. Thornhill is an
epic fantasy and
steampunk writer who
deeply loves her
Savior, and has a

severe addiction to caffeine. She
currently has one novella "The
Lost Descendants" in her fantasy
series "The King and Prophet
Chronicles" which is available in
ebook, print, and also in
audiobook in the near future.

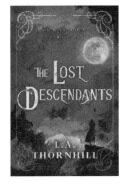

facebook.com/l.a.thornhillauthor

instagram.com/l.a.thornhill

Savannah Jezowski

Savannah Jezowski lives in
a drafty farmhouse in
southern Michigan with
her Knight in Shining
Armor and two wee
warrior princesses. She
specializes in epic fantasy

worlds with
emotional
themes and
characters
that defy the
norm.
"Trickster
Rising" is a
short story in
the *When
Ravens Fall Series.*

Website – www.dragonpenpress.com
Facebook – @savannahjezowskiauthor
Instagram – @savannahjezowskiauthor
Books can be found on Amazon

Ghost in the Thicket
The Night Walkers

Emily Barnett

Emily resides in Colorado with her husband and sons dreaming up magical worlds that feel a bit like home. She is querying a YA fantasy novel and hosts a flash fiction challenge on Instagram every Friday.

www.embarnettauthor.com
www.instagram.com/embarnettauthor

Light

AJ Skelly

AJ Skelly is an author, blogger, and lover of all things fantasy, medieval, and fairy-tale-romance. And werewolves. She has a serious soft spot for them. As an avid life-long reader and a former high school English teacher, she's always been fascinated with the written word. She lives with her husband, children, and many imaginary friends who often find their way into her stories. They all drink copious amounts of

tea together and stay up reading far later than they should.

Books can be purchased wherever books are sold.

Found on social media as AJ Skelly or the Readers of AJ Skelly Facebook Group

and @a.j.skelly on Instagram. Website is www.ajskelly.com

Fading Out

Natalie Noel Truitt

Natalie Noel Truitt is an
aspiring Christian author
who is pursuing a degree in
psychology. She is often on
her front porch drinking a
chai latte, reading a good
book, and hanging out with one of her cats.

You can find her on Instagram: @life_frommydesk.

This Will Not Last

Laurel Jean

Laurel Jean has a passion for
capturing the raw beauty and
emotion of life in words to share
with the world. Some of her
happiest moments are spent chatting
with kindred spirits, playing with
worms on rainy days, and dairy farming with her family in
the Midwest.

Website: <u>laurel-jean.com</u>
Facebook: @laureljeanwriter
Instagram: @laureljean_writer

Scaredy Cat on Halloween Night
Bleached Reminders

Effie Joe Stock

Effie Joe Stock is the
author of The Shadows of
Light series and the
creator of the world Rasa.
You can usually find her
working outside on her
small homestead farm,
playing music, studying
psychology, theology, or
philosophy, running her small
businesses, or riding her dirt bike.
She looks forward to continuing
her publishing dream with the six
books and multiple companion
novels she has written for her epic
fantasy series, along with a few
other works in progress.

Visit Effie Joe Stock Online at www.effiejoestock.com or
follow her on Instagram @effie.joe.stock.author or
YouTube at Effie Joe Stock

Reviewers' Books

If the Broom Fits
by Sarah Sutton

Saving Zora
by Katie Marie

"Your word is a lamp for my feet,
a light on my path."
-Psalm 119:105 (NIV)

Made in the USA
Middletown, DE
12 October 2021